Joshua

5fingers: rescue
The Three Protectors

5fingers book four

°°°°°*12345*°°°°°

Rings on her fingers and bells on her toes,
And she shall have music wherever she goes.

°°°°°*12345*°°°°°

Red Ink. Publishing

Red Ink Publishing Ltd
www.redinkpublishing.co.uk

Also by Joshua Raven

Joshua Raven – 5fingers: rescue

Follow Joshua Raven's blog at www.joshuaraven.com

Twitter: @RavenWrites

Facebook: Joshua Raven Author

Pinterest: Joshua Raven 5fingers

www.5fingers.co.uk

www.redinkpublishing.co.uk

ISBN 978-0-9934011-0-7

Production by JAC Design, Clockhouse Court, Beacon Road,
Crowborough, East Sussex TN6 1AF
Cover design and artwork by Lewis Design
Printed and bound in Great Britain by TJ International Ltd,
Padstow, Cornwall

MIX
Paper from
responsible sources
FSC® C013056

This book is dedicated to my beautiful and talented sister. I will never forget the time we spent as kids, writing a hundred books in crayon and pencil; hearing Tolkien and Shakespeare read to us as pre-schoolers and dancing to rock, punk and pop in the kitchen as teens. You are a vital part of my writing journey, have always been and always will be.

Thanks also to my wonderful 5fingers fans (that includes you!); my supportive wife and children; my editors: Phoebe, Rebekah, Mark and Clare; my friends and supporters at TKC and the CLG; Louis at Lewis Design; Jane and Carole at JAC Design; Jane our inspiring accountant, Naila, Isabelle and Nicole.

Thank you also to anyone involved in these TV and movie productions (which have inspired me to write plot-driven, cinematic fiction) - 24, Alias, Battlestar Galactica, Caprica, West Wing, Nikita, the Alien series, Terminator: The Sarah Connor Chronicles and Dollhouse.

Chapter 1

"Wake up Rach."

"Hmm?"

"Wake up Racoon, you loon."

Plum lipstick. A sneer. A waterfall of raven-black hair. Hands on hips. Black nail varnish.

"Lara?" murmured Rachel. She forced her eyes open. "Is it really you?"

"Of course it's me. Get up. It's time for school."

"School?" Rachel knitted her brow.

"What are you - deaf?"

Rachel let her head loll. She recognised her bedroom. The guitar she never played: propped up against a chair. Her stack of unread books. Posters of her rock heroes, staring moodily.

"Aren't you meant to be in California?" Rachel snuggled further down into her soft duvet.

"Are you tripping, girl?" Lara shot back.

"I don't understand." She realised there was a Lara-shaped hole in her heart. It throbbed like an open wound. Surely Lara had been living in the States for over a year now. Hadn't she? "I miss you," she said.

"Whatever." Lara folded her arms. She slouched against the wall. Her frame melted into a pose, like a mannequin.

"So, you getting up, or what?"

"Hold on a sec. How did you get in?"

"Your dad. Grumpy as ever. A big fat grumpy egg. He's gone off to work by the way. Said he'd be back late tonight."

"Some things never change. Hang on, what colour was his hair?"

"Don't be silly," Lara replied.

"Lara, what colour's his hair?" Rachel was deadpan.

"His hair, Raccoon, is white. Like it's always been."

Rachel sat up quickly. She fixed Lara with her stare. "No, it hasn't."

She caught her breath. Lara stared back at her. If it was even Lara. Was it a demon in disguise like that businessman in the restaurant?

The room seemed to shrink. It was like the two of them were vacuum-sealed in a plastic bag.

"And what colour's my hair?" Rachel demanded.

"Oh, Rach, you goose. Your hair's white as well."

Rachel looked quizzically at her. "Who are you really?"

"It's me: Lara. Otherwise known as Lemur. Mainly by you. And who are you? Come on. Stop being an idiot and get up. We're going to be late! And you know how Mrs Goyle is. She'll chuck us both in detention. Particularly after what happened last time."

"Why? What happened last time?" Rachel scrambled out of bed. She stood up, feeling light-headed. She tried hard to remember. Her memory failed her.

"You know. It was Brad's fault really. It was all his idea. And we went along with it because it was going to be fun, you know. But it made us all really late."

Rachel moved over to her mirror.

"You remember. It was only last term. You asked your mum to cover for you. But she didn't want to lie."

"My what? My mum?" Rachel's puzzled reflection gazed back. It was definitely her.

The face pulled its eyebrows together. Light brown skin. Big brown eyes. Long eyelashes. A dark brown imprint of a hand

8

on her cheek. It looked like a burn. A burn in the shape of five fingers and part of a palm. The Malkin, that hideous pretence of her mother, had marked her. And her hair was a dazzling shade of white.

"But my mum is... My mum's..."

In the reflection, she saw Lara looking blankly at her: waiting. Rachel's eyes darted to her own face again.

"But my mum's dead."

And then she started to remember everything.

°°°°°°*12345*°°°°°°

They all crowded around her body: her father Eddie, the Harcourts – Daniel, Arabella, Cameron and Rory - and Micah, Daniel's assistant.

"All she said was she needed to find the others," Eddie told no one in particular. He wore a grave expression. "She mentioned she was going back to the stone head. Okay, I get that. She needs to be with the others. I get that. The ones who lost their fingers." Eddie waved his hands in exasperation. "But where are they? Is it that place with the purple sky? What's it called? The mezzanine?"

"She also believes we have to stop Samyaza. And I agree with that wholeheartedly," interjected Daniel. "Samyaza has to be stopped. No question."

"I think she was just exhausted. The poor lamb," Arabella mused. "After everything she's been through, what with that monster and everything that happened to her in the other place. She probably didn't tell us the half of it."

"Is she going to die?" Rory asked.

"Of course she's not going to die," Cameron snapped. "Look. She's just asleep."

They watched her chest rising and falling rhythmically. At least she looked peaceful.

Eddie knelt down and stroked Rachel's hair. He gently tried to rock her awake. His frame dwarfed Rachel's petite body. Arabella

9

gently took her wrist, counting the beats of her pulse. Micah went in search of a flannel he could soak in cold water. The kids fidgeted and whispered.

No matter how hard they tried, they couldn't get her to wake up. It was like she'd run away into her mind, into a deep sleep. As though she'd found another portal to go through. But instead of leading to the mezzanine this one took her to a place they couldn't go. A place even further away.

Eddie's house was cramped. The front door opened into the lounge. The seven of them crowded around the sofa peering at Rachel's curled-up body.

Daniel closed his eyes and called on the Dunamis. After a few seconds he opened his eyes.

With an air of authority, he said, "She's going to be fine. The Rescuer knows what is happening. He is with her." He smiled. "She just needs rest. And we need to get some ourselves. I know she's going to be all right."

They visibly relaxed, though Eddie didn't leave Rachel's side. He knelt beside her, stroking her head and back. He looked with sadness down at the scar left by Rachel's encounter with the Malkin.

He took a deep breath. All eyes turned to him.

"I'm sorry, I'm not a very good host," he said without looking up. "My wife was always the one who welcomed people, not me."

Then he glanced at the faces of his new friends. "But I want you to know, you are welcome. I feel like you're my family now. Because of him. The Rescuer. He's done something in me. In my heart."

Daniel nodded in encouragement. Eddie continued. "He brings people closer together, doesn't he? Thank you for caring about my daughter. It means so much to me. My house is your house. Mi casa su casa, and all that. I guess what I want to say is: make yourself at home. Find a chair or bed if you need to. You can even find yourself some food or a drink if you want. I've got plenty of stuff in the fridge and the cupboards. More than enough. Please help yourself, because, well, you see, I don't really cook. There, I've said it. And there's no way I can do food and drinks for seven people."

He pulled a face, making everyone laugh.

"Well, six people," he added, looking into Rachel's face.

"She is going to be fine, Eddie," Daniel reassured him.

"I know," said Eddie softly.

°°°°°12345°°°°°

Rachel started to recall recent events. Her head was full of the mezzanine world. She could clearly picture the violet and magenta sky. The mountains. The crazy forests. The floating rocks. The gaps in the ground that led to nothingness.

She felt the oppression of the demons. Black figures with leathery wings. Small, piercing black eyes. She remembered Zed, that menacing shape shifter who created the Malkin, that hideous thing, and Olm his 'spawner' son. And the caves where she'd found Micah.

The Malkin filled her mind. That nasty imitation of her mother. Its dead eyes and awkward arms. And it spoke to her in her mother's voice. And it burned her. On her face. Her cheek. The horror. Then a huge dragon snatched it up on Griffton beach. The two of them soared into the air. Up, up they went. And gone.

In the next instant, she felt surrounded by mountains. She could picture dazzling white snow. The doorway had opened. They'd used her finger and four others. Technically it was four fingers and a thumb. An ancient evil had spilled out onto the Earth. Samyaza and his Nephilim. The monsters were here. Everything had changed. Danger was everywhere. There was nowhere to hide.

She thought about the five. There were four people like her. Ones who had lost a part of themselves. She longed to join with them. But she didn't know how.

And then she remembered her pool. Rachel's pool. She felt the warm water bathing her body. Washing her clean. In her mind she trod water. The sound of crashing water falling from a height. The pool was deep. She felt at peace.

In her mind's eye she saw the Rescuer King. His face bright. He looked at her with eyes of love. Her heart beat faster, pounding her ribcage. She knew he loved her. She felt the presence of the Dunamis. The power of the Dunamis was inside her. It was the fire in her veins. The Rescuer's Dunamis: the gift he'd given her. She would never be alone again. In the mezzanine, he turned her hair white. Made her new. Stronger.

The voice of the Dunamis came to her. "Are you ready to run again, Rachel, my love?"

"Yes," she answered. "I'm ready." Her words floated around in her head. And in this strange disembodied state, she started to laugh. Hope returned.

She felt like she was falling a great distance. As she had in the mezzanine world. Down and down, bouncing off the ribbons of tiny rocks. Plummeting. Hitting the water far below. Fountains of water thrown into the air.

Rachel opened her eyes and gasped.

"She's awake," Rory cried. His face was right up close to hers. Red cheeks. Huge eyes. Open mouth. A smell of chocolate biscuits.

"She's awake," he yelled. Rachel winced and then laughed.

Chapter 2

"Right. What do we know? What don't we know? And what do we need to do? Anyone?" Daniel asked, taking charge.

"Well, I had a dream, kind of," said Rachel. She was nursing a creamy hot chocolate. The steam caressed her eyelashes: playful ghosts. "Samyaza is loose now. He came out of the mountains: the ones I dream about quite a lot. A bit too much, actually. He's got things with him. Big monsters."

Daniel looked deeply unhappy.

Rachel continued, "It's a bad thing that they're out. When I was in the other place, I saw a monster up close. They're horrible. Black with wings and fangs." She shivered.

"Hmm. Okay. What else?"

"Caleb Noble's not with us. And we really need him," Rachel offered.

"That's right. He stayed behind in the other place, didn't he? With the angel," said Micah thoughtfully. "Mattatron, the Warrior Angel."

"Okay. What else?"

"We met a real life angel. It's July now. That means school's over. Me and Rory miss our friends. Our house has been taken over by baddies. We're homeless now," listed Cameron who was seven and a half – a year and a half older than his brother Rory.

"And it looks like while we were all gone, Griffton turned into a war zone," added Eddie. "I've been back a bit longer than you lot.

I've learned that it's pretty tough for everyone. There are terrorists blowing things up. Everyone's scared. No one really knows what's going on. There were those people on fire. Though that was because of that thing that looked like Rachel's mother."

Rachel winced. "It wasn't mum," she snapped.

"No, chicky. I said it looked like her. I know it wasn't really her." Eddie's voice was soft. Rachel noted that he hadn't called her chicky for years. Kind, tired eyes looked at her from beneath a mass of curly white hair. It was her father and she loved him. Rachel nodded wearily and tried to give him a smile.

"She burned my face," she said quietly. "With her hand. It had my finger sewn onto it along with the others." Rachel stroked her scarred cheek. The pain had gone. A rough indent remained.

"Anything else?" asked Daniel.

"Mobile networks are down and so is the web," said Micah, shaking his head.

"Yup. Anything else?"

"Anything else?" Rory mimicked. Cameron laughed and poked out his tongue at his brother.

"Okay son." Daniel stroked his hair.

They looked at each other for a while. It was warm for July. Uncomfortably warm. Eddie's house needed ventilation.

"There's a lot we don't know," said Arabella. "And we will need to get food soon. And perhaps check on our house and a few of our friends."

"You're right," said Daniel. "There's only so much we're going to find out from here. It's a great base, though. We are more grateful than we can say, Eddie."

Eddie waved his hands and made a face as if to say: "Don't mention it."

"So, anything else?"

"I'd like to go see how Iona is and also the girls at work. And maybe see if Lake's okay." She glanced at Micah, struck, as always, by his beautiful face. His wide jaw, wavy hair and almond-shaped eyes. But they were trained on the floor.

"Good. Me, I need to make a few calls to my business contacts. I also want to check on the house," said Daniel. "Eddie?"

"No, everything that's dear to me is in this room." He put his big arm around Rachel's shoulders. Affection from her father was a new sensation: alien but pleasant. He smelled of lemon body wash: freshly showered. She liked the new Eddie.

°°°°°*12345*°°°°°

Rachel decided to walk over to Iona's house. Nobody wanted her to go on her own but she insisted. She took a small deodorant aerosol with her. If anyone attacked her, she'd spray it right into their eyes.

"Just be safe," said Eddie, giving her yet another hug.

"Okay, Dad. Leave me alone now." She wriggled free.

Russet Road was quiet. A cool breeze washed over her. The bright sunshine belied the mood of the city. It was far too quiet for a weekday. It felt to Rachel like Griffton was sulking in a corner somewhere. It wanted to be left alone.

After a while she came to the wide road that was Roasting Vale Lane. It was a peculiar name for a road, she thought. She knew it came from Middle English. It was made from a couple of Old French words. They referred to a valley where they used to roast stuff. Maybe they roasted meat back in the fourteenth century. Or perhaps the sun was hot like it was today and it was the people who got roasted in the valley. Regardless, Roasting Vale Lane it was, and always had been.

She followed it down to the beach road, Griffton Boulevard, taking in all she saw. There were still signs of the Malkin's attack. Bits of scorched material. Litter from bins that had been kicked over. There was no smell of burning left, though. And the dead people had been removed.

Instead, the air was fresh with the usual healthy pinch of Griffton sea salt. There were very few people around. The ones she saw had their heads down. They avoided any eye contact with her. A few cars drove along the boulevard. But there were nowhere near as many as there should be.

Along the seafront, many of the buildings had been bashed in. Broken panes of glass. Twisted metal. Torn cardboard. Shattered wood. She shook her head. It was disgusting.

As she approached Rock and Shock, her repugnance turned to alarm. All the merchandise was gone. The building was a cavernous maw, exposed to the elements. The racks were mangled, annihilated, obliterated. The counter was gouged. People had thrown their rubbish through the open hole. Drink containers. Dirty rags. Even a deckchair. It was too much.

Fighting back the tears, she forced herself to carry on. "Oh, Rescuer. Help us." She felt the glow of the Dunamis within her, pressing her on.

Rachel passed the Pirate's Paradise. It, too, was a mess. Again, no one was in sight. It was clear that people had enjoyed mutilating her favourite bar. Like the music shop, it was almost unrecognisable. Glass shards glinted in the sand. The furniture had been dragged outside. Left in untidy heaps.

She noticed a shady character hanging around on the beach side of the bar. A man with dark eyes and tangled brown hair. He stared at her, cigarette poking out of a line-mouth.

She kept walking, her eyes on the pavement. A lone seagull circled above.

"Oh, Griffton. What's happened to you?" She sighed.

A cold wind blew. Rachel hugged her body. She noticed, out of the corner of her eye, that the man was following her. He was on the other side of the road. There were no cars on Griffton Boulevard. It was as quiet as a Sunday night.

He crossed over to her side. She quickened her pace. Glancing behind, she saw he was keeping up with her. She brought her shoulders up and her head down, charging ahead. Why didn't he just go away?

She heard him calling out to her, though it was more of a hiss, "Hey girl. Little girl. You lost?"

It wasn't the first time Rachel had been hassled by a stranger. It tended to be evening time, when men had drunk a few pints. It was more unusual to be troubled in the daytime. Her protocol was to ignore him and keep moving.

She was approaching the Tendrils: snaking lanes that spread up through Griffton from the Boulevard. The Tendrils were home to countless boutique shops, delicatessens, diners and outlets selling unusual curios. She breathed in through her nose and ducked into one of them. It was Shelley Lane, a name Rachel liked. A lot of the Tendrils were named after famous poets. Rachel liked this one because of the pun on shells, being a beachside road. She nipped along quickly, hoping the man didn't know the lanes as well as she did.

Without looking back, she turned immediately into an adjacent lane: Donne Close. She knew it had a cut-through to Wordsworth Lane, though it looked like a dead end.

Surrounded by tall residential properties, she went down a narrow lane. Just before she disappeared, she looked back. There was no sign of the man.

Wordsworth Lane led back around to Griffton Boulevard, via Marvell Lane. Before she stepped out onto the main road, she peered sneakily around the corner. She couldn't see any people either way. The man had most likely followed her into the Tendrils and kept going north.

Rachel walked quickly along Griffton Boulevard, looking back every so often. A solitary seagull flew in from the sea. It made a loud screeching noise. Fortunately, that was her only companion. The sun punched through the misty clouds. It brushed her face with warmth, feeling like melted butter on toast.

At last, she made it to Iona's house. At least her building looked intact, thought Rachel. She tried ringing the doorbell. No response. She tapped briskly on the front door: three times with her knuckles. That should get Iona's attention. It was a good, solid, wooden door. You'd have to be pretty strong to kick that down. Still nothing. She glanced over her shoulder. Still clear of people.

She tried calling out. "Iona. Are you in there? It's me, Rachel. Iona?"

She wasn't confident her friend was in. Or if she was even alive. Anything could happen these days. She tried looking through the windows. The net curtains were closed and she couldn't see anything. Rachel turned to leave.

Just then, she heard a clicking sound inside. The door opened slowly, and her good friend peered out. As soon as she saw Rachel, she heaved the door the rest of the way and swept her up in a huge embrace.

"Oh, Rachel. I've been so scared," she sobbed, her big hair engulfing both herself and Rachel. "It's been a nightmare. Everything's a nightmare."

°°°°°*12345*°°°°°

A fight was kicking off at the local supermarket down the road from Eddie's house. Micah was trying to decide whether to intervene. Arabella shrank back. Cameron and Rory stood with their mouths wide open.

Two women in dirty clothes fought over a loaf of bread. One tried to bite the other. Onlookers watched, looking bored. Most people ignored the two and carried on shopping.

There were very few fresh items on sale. The white cob loaf they were fighting over was one of them. It was a large, rock-shaped object that could be used to club someone to death. Arabella hoped it wouldn't come to that.

She had picked up some vegetables, her basket guarded fiercely by Micah. They looked like they were past their sell-by date but they had to suffice. The boys found some fresh fruit that was hidden underneath a stack of empty crates. Arabella buried these under a couple of packs of flour tortilla wraps. It was clear they needed to hold onto what they had.

She exchanged glances with Micah. He shrugged and nodded

to the checkout. They only had a basketful of things but it would have to be enough. Besides, Eddie had more food and drinks back at the house which he'd recently stored up. He'd had a sense things were heading this way. The Dunamis had prompted him and in obedience, he'd acted. As it turned out, it was a highly practical move. Citizens always bought everything in sight when a crisis hit. A fuel shortage. Flooding. Snow. You name it. So, he'd filled his shed with tins and long-life items. Now he had a family with kids living with him, it all made sense.

°°°°°12345°°°°°

After hugging her for a long time, Iona led Rachel through to the hall. She hobbled in front of her on her broken leg, leaning against the wall for support.

"You're the first person I've seen in days," Iona said. Looking back at Rachel she rolled her eyes dramatically.

"Really?"

"Well, almost. Lake came by. Before all the bad things happened."

"My Lake?"

"Your Lake? That's not what he said," Iona retorted. "He told me you two had split up."

"Really?"

"Come in. Have a seat. And please ignore the mess." There were piles of dirty plates and cutlery on the kitchen surfaces. It was most unlike Iona.

"Thanks." Iona pulled out a cyan-coloured bar stool. Rachel followed her lead and perched on the edge of another one. She rested her arms on the counter.

"So, you haven't split up?"

"Well, we kind of have, I think. Actually, I'm not sure we've actually split up-split up."

"He showed me your note, Rachel. I hope you don't mind me saying this, but that was a bit harsh. I mean, I dumped a guy by

19

text once. And that was bad enough! But we hadn't been going out for long. Not like you guys. Anyway. It was different. He was a real jerk."

"Hold on Iona. What are you talking about?"

"The note you sent him. You know? The one saying you needed a break and were going up to the Midlands to stay with your family?"

Rachel's voice climbed an octave. "What note? I didn't send any note. That wasn't me!"

Iona gave her best 'calm down' expression.

"All right. It did seem a bit strange to me. And out of character. Although to be honest, I wouldn't put anything past you. No offence. You seem to live with a lot of - how can I put this - secrets."

"Thanks a lot."

"I mean, it was written how you'd write it," said Iona, sheepishly.

"Let's forget about the note. It was probably written by that wretched Kumiko."

"Not her." Iona looked to the ceiling. There was a long silence. "By the way, I like what you've done with your hair. It's a start. But when are you going to put some colour in it? What shade are you going for? I could do it for you, you know."

"I like it the way it is. Anyway, there's a story behind it."

"Do tell! But I want you to know we are coming back to Mister Emerson later on. I need to know everything."

"If we must."

Rachel reflected for a moment. She stared past Iona's shoulder at the kitchen drainer. So much had happened since she last saw her friend.

"First, tell me about yourself. When did you get out of hospital? Have you been outside?"

"Oh, I got better a week ago. I've been trying to stay indoors. I don't really like politics, but I know there hasn't been an official change in government. I would have got a voting form and all that. But it's bad out there. There has been a big change. People seem to have taken over the city. Bad people."

"Who?"

"They say they're here to protect us, but I have my doubts. They've got their own police force. Guys in leather outfits. Like those terrible heavy metal music videos from the Nineties. They're locking down parts of Griffton. People go missing. And that Kumiko girl – I'm sure it's her – well, it looks like her anyway: she's their spokesperson. I saw her on TV. Same face, kind of. And things are still getting blown up."

"Blown up?"

"Don't you know? There were terrorist attacks on City Hall, the police headquarters, and an army place. Then there were bus bombs. Nowhere's safe. They even smashed up Rock and Shock. Poor Ben can't live there anymore because the windows have all been broken. So he's taken to sleeping on his friends' couches. But not here, mind you."

"Who would do such a thing?"

"It's these people who follow the Rescuer and the Dynamos, or whatever. They're pure evil. I don't know what they want but they don't care about human life."

Rachel sat up straight. She looked Iona full in the face. "Tell me everything that's happened since I've been gone. Tell me slowly. And don't miss anything out," she demanded.

Chapter 3

"This garbage you've given me is totally unacceptable. You are a terrible writer," Kumiko snarled. "Do it all again. And this time keep to the brief," she thundered. "I really don't know why I brought you on board."

Lake Emerson shrank under her ferocity. The past few days, she had changed completely towards him. A one hundred and eighty degree turn. Like a roller-blader's power-slide where you end up facing in the other direction, thought Lake.

He was sure he'd read the situation right. Didn't she ask him to come and work with her and live in the big house? The two of them? It was definitely her idea for him to leave the paper. He didn't really want to because all his friends were there. And it was walking distance from home. But she had convinced him with the promise of money and fame. So, he'd departed from the Griffton News with a mixture of sorrow and elation and a hundred questions from the reporters. They clearly thought he'd lost his mind. Perhaps they were right.

Things were fine to start with. Kumi spent time with him, hanging out. She even allowed him to kiss her once. It was late one evening. The Dream Fighters had all gone off to a meeting in the basement so there wasn't anyone around. He'd enjoyed that one evening but it was an isolated event.

How quickly things had shifted. Now, she hated the sight of him. He was starting to wonder what he ever saw in her. She was harder work than Rachel and that was saying something.

Rachel, he thought. Rachel. Her ocean-sized eyes filled his mind. Deep, dark pools. And her lovely little ears.

"Are you listening to me?" snapped Kumi.

"Hmm?"

"You're pathetic." She turned her back on him and marched out of his office.

From the corridor she called out, "I have to go to London now. Back late. Have the next draft on my desk by the end of the day."

With tears in his eyes, Lake screwed the paper into a ball and threw it towards the metal bin. It landed amongst the other crumpled sheets, like desperate jumpers leaping from a burning building.

Lake's office was hidden away in the maze of bedrooms, dressing rooms and offices, upstairs at Lytescote Manor. Dark hardwood furniture filled the place and made the air smell musty and ancient. The decor seemed appealing at first. He loved the aristocratic shades of brown and all the tiny gold touches. Now, a week or so on, it just oppressed him.

"I can't work like this," he whispered to his monitor screen. "She's crazy! What did I see in her?" He threw his hands up and clasped them behind his head, gripping his treacle-coloured hair.

He knew he would try to escape if he could. But guards were everywhere. He could see them out on the lawn. They trained up and down the long driveway. Drills and marches, sprints and target practice. The metal gates were constantly opening and closing, breathing these nasty warriors out over Griffton like so many dirty germs. But he wasn't permitted to pass through them.

And all the while they wanted him to write favourable articles explaining their new world order. His job was to reassure people through the written word.

Whoever read his stuff anyway? Web access was patchy at best. It was down to the bombings and the public disorder. Sometimes the internet was down for hours at a time. And he never saw any paper versions of what he produced. Was his writing actually getting published? Where was his fame? He was stuck in a nightmare. One pointless day followed another. He imagined it stretching into weeks, months and years. Kumi was always busy so he spent hours on his own, working, reading or sleeping.

Meanwhile, a feeling deep down in his gut told him that every day he stayed here, he was adding to the darkness this place produced through its very existence. This was a factory of gloom: a monstrosity. He had to escape.

°°°°°*12345*°°°°°

"Iona, what they've been telling you is all wrong. They're lying."

"What do you mean?"

"Look. It's not the followers of the Rescuer who are blowing things up."

"I'm listening." Iona swept back her wavy hair, pulling at it with her fist. She produced a hair-tie from somewhere and tamed her mass of curls. She looked thoughtfully at Rachel.

"I know you think I'm crazy and that's fine. Frankly, I'm used to it."

"No, what you say does make some sort of sense. It seems a bit convenient that these people were ready to save the day, even before the bombings."

"You have to believe me, Iona," Rachel blurted out, staring. "I met the King of the world – the Rescuer. He's all about living, not killing."

"I don't know what you mean."

Rachel knew how insane she sounded but the words tumbled out of her regardless. "He takes all the bad out of you and makes you new. Don't ask me how. All the stuff you're ashamed of thinking. All the bad stuff you've ever done and you're sorry about, deep down. And he's beautiful. His face shines like the sun. And he did this to my hair." Rachel ran her fingers through her white tresses.

"Okay," smiled Iona, glazing over a little.

"He gave me weapons that aren't like killing weapons. He gave me faith and joy – laughter! I can laugh now. Properly! I don't have to be miserable all the time. Not anymore."

"Rachel, you're making no sense to me. At all," admitted Iona.

"And he gave me his Dunamis. His power. I carry him now. I carry his presence in me."

Iona shook her head slowly as if to say: "You've lost me."

Rachel sighed and looked down at her hands. Then she perked up. The Dunamis had whispered an idea into her mind. She said cheerily, "Would you like to meet him?"

Almost before her brain could catch up with her mouth, Iona said, "Sure."

Rachel took a deep breath, placed her hand on her friend's bare arm and closed her eyes. Iona's skin was cool under her fingers. Iona gasped and Rachel suddenly felt her friend's arm heat up where she touched her. It was as though warmth flowed through the palm of her right hand. It was like a cool, metal radiator shifting from cold to warm then hot as the water flooded the channels inside.

Iona began to shake gently as the Dunamis poured his love and power into her. "I see," she said, softly. And then again, "I see now." Iona smiled. The pain in her leg went. She started to weep quietly.

"I must tell Ben," she said softly. He has to know about this. And Mum and Dad. If only they knew."

°°°°°*12345*°°°°°

"I need to get out of here," Lake told himself, stuffing clothes into his rucksack. "These are bad people, and I've been an idiot."

He went to his en suite bathroom. It had fawn-coloured marble tiles and panels made of white-painted wood. Early-evening light filtered in as he clawed toiletries into his material wash bag. He hastily zipped it closed.

It was the end of his work day, six o'clock. Dressed in a T-shirt and combat trousers, he pulled on his trainers and chucked his bag over his shoulder.

Fortunately, he'd only brought a few sets of clothes with him. He kept everything else back at his parents' house. He reasoned that he could always go back. Of course, at the time, he didn't realise they were going to keep him prisoner at Lytescote Manor.

And so he made do with what he had and what he was given: a bath-robe and towel and some other bits and pieces. Back in his room, he left a set of novels he'd found there and some spare pyjamas from Kumiko. He didn't want to take anything he didn't own.

So, with a quick glance back to check he hadn't left anything important, he fled the room. In the corridor outside, he passed a couple of Dream Fighters. Bulky, dusty men. They were deep in conversation, though they stopped as he passed. He tried not to breathe in the smell of body odour and old leather.

The warriors still gave him the creeps. They were always so focused on being Dream Fighters. They swore like the troopers they were, and trained incessantly. Sometimes, they fought with each other in the house and outside it. They frequently broke a table or a vase in the process.

Apart from that, they didn't seem to do much else. They didn't appear to have much personality. They definitely lacked a sense of humour. He'd tried his best jokes on them. Not even a smile. Plus, they obeyed Kumiko without question. Sometimes they called her 'Master', which Lake found eccentric. But then again, Mistress would be equally weird.

Lake had a thin layer of sweat on his brow. No one stopped him going downstairs. As far as they were concerned, he was carrying his washing to the laundry room in the basement. He'd done it before. It was none of their business and they didn't want to fall foul of Kumiko – or the one she represented. Samyaza.

In his hand he clutched a few sheets of paper with his final draft of the press release printed on it. But, of course, it wasn't really his final draft. No, this was a message to Kumiko telling her, in very clear and basic language, what he thought about his so-called job.

He descended two flights to the ground floor. The stairs were lit by a stained glass window that displayed the coat of arms of Henry the Eighth. It overlooked the internal courtyard. There was no time to admire it.

At the bottom, he turned left and walked down the oak-floored corridor. It led to Kumi's office on the east side of the house.

The heavy wooden door was ajar and there were no guards in sight. Beyond dropping his farewell note on her desk, he didn't have any further plans. He could try to walk out the front door and use his mouth to talk his way past the security team. It hadn't worked the last couple of times he'd tried, but you never know. Third time's a charm.

The office had a timbered ceiling and impressive fireplace. There were ancient books on the shelves with gold and green lettering. He glanced around the room to check that Kumi really had left and wasn't hiding. Then he dragged the door closed behind him.

Feeling bold, he pulled the leather chair out and sat down. He put his feet up on the old wooden desk, dropped the note in the middle of it, right on her jotter pad, and grinned.

Just then, a sound came from the fireplace. Lake swung his chair around and saw a panel opening up at its base. It was a thick stone square, hinged at the front. Lake gasped as a man emerged. His throat constricted; panic washing over him.

It wasn't a Dream Fighter or a monster. It was the businessman, Daniel Harcourt: the owner of the house. He recognised the sharp nose and wire-frame glasses. He also saw something that looked like a gun. Lake opened his mouth. "Don't hurt me!" he yelped.

"Keep quiet," whispered Daniel. "Please."

Lake carried on staring with his mouth gaping open but nodded anyway.

"How many men are there in my house?" Daniel demanded in a quick, hushed tone. He wore a blue, button-down shirt. His hair was unkempt.

"I don't know. Maybe forty or fifty. Something like that."

Daniel came out, leaving the trap door open. He bent down low to avoid bashing his skull on the hard brickwork. Lake guessed he'd done this before.

"Have they broken much?"

"I don't think so. Sometimes they, you know, wrestle and stuff gets smashed by accident."

Daniel looked unhappy.

"Is it just you?"

"What do you mean?"

"Escaping today."

Lake looked puzzled.

"You have your bag with you."

"Yup. I'm on my own."

"Not anymore, Lake."

Daniel walked over to the desk: his desk, Lake presumed. He felt underneath it with his fingers and pressed a button.

"What's that?" asked Lake, but the question hung in the air. Daniel smiled a grim smile in return and said, "Okay, done."

He added, "Are you coming or going?"

"Is Rachel okay?" Lake stammered.

"Of course she is."

"You know where she is?"

"We can't hang around here chatting. Come with me or stay. But if you choose to stay I will have to kill you."

"Really?"

There was no humour in Daniel's expression.

"Fine. I'm coming. I've had enough here anyway. I mean it's a nice house and all, but..."

"Okay. Let's go."

Daniel pushed Lake in front of him and climbed in after.

He said quietly, "In answer to your question, that button I pressed electrifies the water tank and the door handles. Oh, and the toilet seats. I call it my 'surprise house party'."

He carefully pulled the slab down over his head using a metal handle. It made a dull thud as it closed.

Lake found himself in a long brick tunnel, illuminated by Daniel's flashlight.

"This way," said the businessman.

Chapter 4

Wearing black lipstick and a sneer, Kumiko stared at the group of Dream Fighters. She had assembled them in the high-ceilinged entrance hall to Lytescote Manor. They stood to attention in their bulky armour, waiting. Ornate, recessed lights lit the broad, impressive chamber.

Forty eyes looked impassively at Kumiko: twenty fighting men, standing in two rows of ten. They were like tight springs ready to uncoil at a moment's notice. All she had to say was the word.

She had returned to the house late that night. She worked everything out pretty quickly. It was obvious. Lake had gone. Betrayal stabbed her heart: a shard of ice that no one could remove. Involuntarily, she winced as she thought about it.

His room had been her first stop. Packed up. No Lake. Trying to stay calm, she went to her room and put away her motorcycle helmet and leathers. She made time to get herself a cold drink. Next she went to her office and saw the note. Somehow she remained composed.

Stewing all the while, she turned the conundrum over in her mind about the missing Lake Emerson. It was pretty clear to her. His things were gone. He was gone. He had left a vitriolic note. It was patently clear to her. He'd done a runner right under the noses of her men. But how had he escaped? Through a window? Up a chimney? They were completely incompetent. Somebody was going to pay.

She turned it over in her mind and eyed the soldiers, coolly. The huge front door was behind her. The wall in front was a chequerboard of wide, dark-wood panels. An antique painting stretched upwards above the warriors' heads. It was an oil-on-canvas scene of the Prince Regent riding his horse through the browns, greens and blues of the countryside. In the background was a hint of water. It was made up of delicate horizontal strokes of silver, white and blue paint, if one cared to look closely at it. Personally, Kumiko hated the picture.

The room was broad, wide and tall. But the combination of ancient wood, unwashed men and insufficient ventilation made it smell musty. Stifling. One of the Dream Fighters fidgeted in his leather uniform. He made a rustling sound as he moved his torso. A bead of perspiration formed on his brow. Regardless, he continued to stare ahead.

Kumiko's face contorted. She was no longer able to keep her anger in check. It was like trying to keep a lid on an over-packed suitcase. The time had come for its contents to spill out.

Without any warning she hurled her glass across the room. It detonated as it made impact with the base of the painting behind the Dream Fighter's head. Shards of glass ricocheted back at his neck. A true soldier, he didn't flinch. The glass left a rip at the bottom of the painting: ruining the delicately-painted water. Nobody paid any attention.

"No one saw him leave? None of you? He just walked down the drive and out through the security gates?" she screamed.

"We don't know for certain that he's gone, Miss Starkweather," volunteered one of the Dream Fighters bravely. He had a thick accent of uncertain origin. It might have been Indian or Nepalese. Kumiko didn't care.

She flew at him, swiping her long nails across his face. A shriek came from her throat, and her eyes blazed. He jerked his hand up to his cheek as the blood started to appear.

Nobody came to his rescue. The men knew their place. She was their commander: their Master Samyaza's representative. She was untouchable. They were soldiers for Samyaza: war or peace, the pay's the same. Today, it was war and the bullets were flying.

Just as quickly as she had flared up, she grew restful again. Psychotically tranquil, perhaps. She turned her head to stare at the man she'd attacked, eyebrows raised, and smiled.

"Oh, he's gone," she stated. She tightened her lips and continued to look at him as he clutched his face. Still calm, Kumiko added, "He might still be in the house, hiding up a chimney. He might be stuck in the bathroom. He might have turned into a bat. But he hasn't. Trust me. He's gone. His rucksack's gone and he left a note on my desk saying he was escaping."

"Oh," said one of the men.

"Oh, indeed. But just in case, I want you to split up and search the house again. Top to bottom. In the unlikely event that you do find him, beat him up. Break some bones. I don't care. Me? I'm going to my office. I need to think. If any of you geniuses has another brainwave, come and find me. And for the love of Samyaza, will someone fix the electrics, please? We've had enough shocks for one night. And I need the toilet."

As she walked to her office, she muttered, "I should never have given him the job. I never liked him anyway." The rest was slander and cursing.

At the entrance to her office she met the Sapana Commander.

"You," she snapped, giving him a dark, brooding look. "Do you know the Griffton News?"

"Of course, Miss Starkweather," he replied in a low voice.

"Burn it down. The whole building. Burn it to the ground. That'll teach him."

"Right away, Master."

ooooo12345ooooo

Sitting in her office chair, Kumiko stared at the bookcases. They lined the walls of the office. Daniel Harcourt really loved books, she thought. She didn't share his hobby though.

Behind her lay the empty fireplace, the log basket sitting unemployed on the hearth. It was one of those wide affairs with a thick wooden beam on the top. On the mantelpiece above the fireplace was a line of ornaments from around the world. A brown and green wooden frog instrument. A small black skull. A jade lighthouse. A tiny chessboard. Above these was a broad ladder of shelves that housed even more books. Their dark spines stared at Kumiko from all around her.

She decided she hated old books. She considered having a book burning party. Books sneer at you that they know more than you. They taunt you with their knowledge. The show-offs. Besides, who has time to read anymore? "I'm going to burn you," she announced. She pulled one tall tome off the shelf. It was a book on art history. In disgust, she threw it onto the floor. It made a satisfying thud. The impact dented its golden spine and made her smile briefly.

She screamed long and hard. The wood and paper muffled the noise but it rang in her ears. Then she cried, dissolving into deep sobs. Her body rose up and down as they racked her frame. She was physically wrecked with all the travelling and long nights, the meetings and the decisions. Everywhere she went she met agents of the new order. Murderers. Torturers. Destroyers. They were her people. Her gang. She knew it was all necessary so she could build the sort of world Samyaza had described to her. The one he waxed lyrical about. One where they were in charge and everyone danced to their tune. They would be the highest authority and would bow to no one. Then finally she could rest.

But mentally she was at her capacity. She needed sleep and respite but was unlikely to find it. She was at an emotional low ebb, strung out, desperate, lost. Broken. Lake leaving was the last straw. The icicle of betrayal protruded from her heart.

"Sammy. I need you, my love. When are you coming?"

"Soon, my dear Kumiko. Soon," said the suntanned surfer dude, nestled in the depths of her spirit.

He was so real to her, but not quite real enough for her to embrace. How she longed for him. He smiled a wide and handsome smile. His deep brown eyes regarded her under thick eyebrows. Black hair tumbled to his shoulders in gentle waves. She gazed at his soft honey-brown cheeks, specked with bristle. His peaceful demeanour made her feel stronger. He poured his strength into her and she lapped it up.

"You're perfect," she sighed. "Perfect for me."

"And you are my queen. We will rule the world together."

"That is so good to hear. That I'm not alone. I could really do with your help, Sammy. He's gone. I'm sorry. The reporter, Lake. He escaped. I don't know how or where, but I'll get to the bottom of it."

"It is of little concern. Easy come, easy go. In the grand scheme of things, it amounts to very little, whether he is with us or not. He was your toy, not mine."

"I'm glad to hear you say that."

"We have larger matters to consider. How is the programme going?"

"The media one or the country campaign?"

"The tech campaign. Is it ready? Are the prisoners all accounted for?"

"Yes, they've run the final tests on the chip now. Doctor Sullington's ready to start implanting. He's preparing the facility for mass manufacture and rollout."

"That is good news. Keep me posted. I'm on my way. Not long now. We will be together soon."

"Can't wait."

Kumiko turned to her mobile. She keyed in a quick text to Doctor Sullington and sat back, exhausted. There was always so much work to do. It was endless.

°°°°°12345°°°°°

Sebastian Gomme was a law court official. No one special. But he did an important job. He didn't know why he'd been chosen. They took him in the middle of the night. It made no sense to him. Why him and not his wife? She was also in the law. A magistrate. And why kidnap them and not mistreat them? It made no sense.

There were plenty of books to read and a little food to eat once or twice a day. It wasn't gruel either but bread and vegetables.

They kept the prisoners in an underground army facility on the west of Griffton. It was the one that had been bombed previously. Above ground the building was ruined. Broken walls stood like jagged grey teeth. However, the lower floors were intact. Reinforced with concrete and metal.

The prisoners spent many days in the cell block. The nights were cold. The mattresses were thin. Captives often sobbed through the night and even the day. Guards were everywhere. They said they worked for the Rescuer. The people who bombed the city. Curse them and their filthy ideology. Perhaps the soldiers were keeping everyone safe underground. Was it even worse above ground? But the men didn't answer questions. Sebastian eventually gave up asking.

He spoke to a number of people in the adjoining cells. A newspaper editor called Mike. He wasn't there for long. They led him away. Then there was a head teacher called Edith. A policeman called Abdul. Nobody knew what was going on. They'd all left behind spouses, partners, children, friends. But equally, those people might also have been taken and held somewhere else. Nobody wanted to think about the fact they might be dead. Keep hope alive, they told each other.

Today, everything changed. They got taken to a large building near the cliff. They were transported handcuffed and blindfolded on a series of coaches, at a guess. The sound of diesel engines. Heavy gear changes. The road crunching under fat tyres.

Sebastian was weary. Plus he'd grown used to the sight of men in armour. They guarded them. Then they bound them. They looked like a formidable force. Fighting wasn't an option. Nor was breaking for freedom. They carried swords and knives for goodness sake.

The people of Griffton were herded like cattle into a building. The blindfolds were removed. Sebastian saw he was with many hundreds of other prisoners. Perhaps bordering a thousand people. Their clothes were dusty and dirty, creased and dull. That's what happens when you live and sleep in the same threads, he thought.

They stood, blinking, in an office block, hotel or factory, it wasn't clear. Sebastian found the entrance hall spectacular, impressive, bewildering. It was reminiscent of a five-star hotel lobby. Or perhaps a six or seven star one. Like in Dubai or Abu Dhabi. It had sparkling white-tiled floors and glass panels everywhere. Armed soldiers edged the walls, their faces impassive.

Soldiers encircled them. Subdued, the people looked at each other with wet eyes. Whispering every so often. One young man tried to run for the doors. He had a strong jaw and piercing blue eyes. He was restrained easily by two soldiers in their Medieval outfits. One punched him sharply in the stomach. Then they carried him away. He didn't resist. No one else tried anything clever. These were the new masters. Brutal, oppressive, controlling.

Sebastian realised he was being pushed towards a big elevator. He shuffled along with a dozen others. They were accompanied by two guards. It was a snug fit in the cage. Metal doors closed. The lift descended.

The doors opened revealing another huge room. It looked like a ballroom with chandeliers but no windows. Dazzling white light bathed the crowd. Blue, furry carpet lined the walls. They were ushered in.

The men in charge, the fearsome hosts, started to circulate. They were armed and confident. Black and brown tunics. Red or brown sashes. An array of swords: broad, long, fat-handled, slim. They eyed their captives and grunted, making everyone uncomfortable.

They led the prisoners individually out to a room at the far end of the hall. Sebastian shuffled along reluctantly with a few others. They swapped names quietly: Sally, Chen, Abigail, Gordon and Rodney. No one dared to talk freely. They saw what happened to the man who tried to run.

The next room was nondescript: a corporate meeting room in neutral colours. Once there, they were asked separately to move to a curtained-off area at the back of the room. One by one they did as they were told.

A man in a suit introduced himself as Doctor Sullington. He had a sizable white beard, thick white hair on either side of a bald egghead, and thick black glasses. Sebastian wondered if he was friendly and tried to connect. Only, the doctor's eyes were blank and his pupils were hard and black. He was definitely not friendly. More professional than amiable. Officious.

He shook Sebastian's hand and said firmly that he was assigning him a new name. It was a single syllable, Uz. Afterwards, Sebastian would find it hard to recall. However, the doctor made a note of it on a tablet.

"What do you mean by my 'new' name?"

But the doctor was keen to move on. He ushered Sebastian forcefully through to the next stage and his question hung in the air.

Behind the curtain, a muscular male nurse injected the back of his neck using a large medical instrument. He assumed it was a nurse. It may just have been one of his captors dressed in a white hospital uniform instead of a soldier's tunic like the others.

"Ow!" he complained.

"This is your chip. For your own good. The sting will go in a bit," the 'nurse' explained in a gruff voice. His voice was robotic. Sebastian imagined he had repeated the same mantra all day. His eyes were also blank. They say the eyes are the windows to the soul. Not in this man's case, thought Sebastian.

"You leave through there. The lift takes you to street level. Then you're free to go. Head south for the city. Next?"

Cupping the back of his neck in his left palm, Sebastian wandered down to the elevator in a daze. Before he departed, he looked back at the nurse and saw he also had a red mark at the base of his neck.

Chapter 5

They started at the top of the house, investigating the attic space. Being late at night, they turned on all the lights they could find. They searched slowly and carefully because there were many hidey holes up there. But the prisoner hadn't climbed his way into the attic.

Next they combed through all the rooms on the second floor. Rooms they used as barracks. And there are many, many rooms in Lytescote Manor on every floor, so it took time. They looked inside the wardrobes and behind doors. They looked under the beds and in the bathrooms, checking behind shower curtains. They even looked in the chimneys as Kumiko suggested. The men paired up in order to do it as quickly as possible. They carefully checked Kumiko's bedroom – Daniel and Arabella's former chamber. Their search was careful, so as not to make their leader unhappy. But it still involved rifling through her personal space. The four-poster bed. The en suite bathroom. Her walk-in wardrobe. But the escapee wasn't there.

They worked their way down the house, back through the second floor and then onto the first. On the ground floor, their search stretched from the front of the house through the dining and living rooms. They investigated the kitchens and breakfast room, the orangery and the back rooms. No sign of him.

A group went down into the basement and they combed the storerooms. They checked the meeting room where they gathered to commune with Samyaza. The laundry and boiler rooms and additional kitchen were also empty.

Meanwhile Dream Fighters went outside and marched through the gardens and the driveway which were lit up by the house and driveway lights. They used the moonlight to look further down the drive into any trees that were climbable.

They went into the octagonal gatehouse to check up there. Climbing the staircase they peered into the rooms. But still, he was nowhere to be seen. Some of the Dream Fighters went into the fields but these were clear. Even the grass was asleep.

Most of the soldiers who were originally stationed at the house had moved on to the army barracks, or taken other positions in the city. Only one remained who remembered the escape route from Daniel Harcourt's office: the one that went down through the base of the fireplace.

The memory came to this young Dream Fighter while he was looking under the billiard table in the games room. He quickly told his commanding officer who moved quickly to the office where Kumiko sat. The young soldier followed him.

The commander rapped quickly on the door.

"Yes?" said Kumiko wearily.

"Master, permission to enter?"

"Come in. Have you found him? I want to get to bed."

"We think we know how he left the house," said the officer. "This soldier knows of a way."

"Tell me." Her arms were folded and she stared; her mouth a line.

The commander nodded for his junior to go forward. The young Dream Fighter moved over to the fireplace. He took a long look at it. Then he grabbed the front of the low metal grate that lined the base of the fireplace. Only it wasn't a grating. It was a handle. He lifted up the stone slab, which was on a hinge. A rectangular hole led downwards into the darkness. "Aha. Clever, clever," sang Kumiko in a breathy voice. "So, he left through my office! Clever Lakey."

The Dream Fighter Officer felt able to laugh a little himself.

There was a note on the top step which the soldier gingerly picked up.

Kumiko roared: "He left through my office!" Her eyes blazed. Her face was a boiling planet: storm clouds racing over the surface.

The young Dream Fighter flinched. He was in two minds about whether or not to give Kumiko the note. But it was too late. She spied it and snatched it out of his hand with a curt: "give me that".

"Now get out, both of you!" she screamed. "Come back with twenty soldiers. I want you to flush him out of that tunnel right now."

Reluctantly, she unfolded the note and read it.

"My wife and I want our house back. Consider this your eviction notice. And tell Samyaza he can go to hell. Sincerely, Daniel William Harcourt."

Kumiko threw back her head and screamed.

°°°°°*12345*°°°°°

On the car journey away from Lytescote Manor, Lake caught up with his dad, Blake. The mobile phones were working momentarily, though there was an annoying crackle on the line.

"Are you all right, son?" His father's deep voice brought tears to his eyes.

"Yeah Dad. Just about. Mum okay?"

"We're fine. How's your government job going? Are they looking after you in your new digs?"

"Government?"

"They're the ones in charge now, aren't they? So, you're working for the government."

"That's one way of looking at it. To be honest, Dad, I never should have left the Griffton News."

"Why's that then?"

"It's a long story. I'll try and pop by soon to fill you in. And I also need to grab some fresh clothes."

"It would be great to see you, son. Just stay safe."

"I'll try my best. Oh, Dad, one more thing. If anyone asks about me, you don't know where I am."

"But I don't know where you are."

"That's great. Make sure you tell them that. Bye Dad."

Lake put his mobile on standby.

He was in the back of a filthy private taxi with Daniel. The driver had a low forehead, a single thick eyebrow and coal-black stubble. He communicated by grunting.

At their feet was a rats' nest of empty cartons, cigarette packets, old newspapers and plastic bags.

"So, let me get this straight. They took over your house and ran you out. They're really the bad guys. So, that makes you one of the good guys?"

"Correct so far," said Daniel.

"But you're with the Rescuer's lot. And the Dunamis. You blew up those buildings. Why would you do that?"

"Wake up Lake. You got played. They lied to you."

Lake furrowed his brow and looked thoughtfully at his hands. "Is Rachel really with you?"

"My family and I are staying at her house at the moment. Her dad's hosting us for the time being."

"Eddie? You know, Eddie? And he's being, like, nice? This is Rachel's dad we're talking about, right?"

"You will find Mr Race a changed man."

Lake scoffed, "This I want to see."

But beneath his bold exterior, Lake felt anxious about seeing Rachel again. Her farewell note had seared itself into his brain. They were no longer a couple. She had made her choice. But then again, so had he. He had chosen Kumiko, and he really wished he hadn't.

ooooo*12345*ooooo

Arabella was frowning at her mobile phone. She sat on the sofa with Rachel. Every so often, they heard a sound from the boys playing upstairs. It was generally a squeal from a tickle or a thud from a tumble.

Eddie was sorting out the food with Micah down in the garden shed. They had cans, packets, cartons and tubes. It kept them occupied until Daniel returned.

Brahms melodies hovered around the front room. Arabella had found Eddie's music and alighted on the Violin Concerto in D. At times the melody, an allegro non troppo, reached the ceiling. At others it was as though the notes lay heavily on the ground like thick snow.

Rachel smiled. It was such a pleasure to introduce the Rescuer and his Dunamis to Iona. It blew her world apart in a good way. Plus the Rescuer completely healed her leg. That was amazing. There were no words for what happened. Iona wept and wept, overwhelmed, thankful, relieved. On leaving, she promised she would try to stay in close touch with Rachel. They were sisters now. Sisters in spirit.

Rachel's house looked tidy and spacious. Like it used to when her mum was alive. Arabella was amazing. She liked to tidy as she waited. She even found the vacuum cleaner. As well as restoring order, Arabella managed to bring out the colours in the house.

As the summer sun reached through the windows, Rachel felt like she was sitting in a Disney film. Arabella looked like a Disney Princess, pale and serene with her long brown hair tied in a French plait.

"I have something I need to tell you, Rachel," she said, in polite, clipped tones. Rachel loved her posh accent.

"Daniel is on his way back from the house. He has your friend with him."

Rachel looked up at her and paid attention.

"He has Lake with him," she said emphatically.

Rachel gasped. Arabella waited patiently.

"Would you like to talk? We have about twenty minutes until they arrive."

Rachel nodded.

°°°°°*12345*°°°°°

"The web connection's still pretty bad, but calls and texts are okay," Eddie said as he walked through from the back door.

Micah came in after him, looking flushed. Rachel had almost got used to how beautiful he was, though it still caught her by surprise on occasion. He'd made it clear earlier on that he really wasn't interested in dating anyone - not that she'd asked him directly. She was rabidly curious, though. Here he was: a handsome and unattached guy with almond-shaped eyes and perfect teeth. He appeared to like the company of females. Her company in particular, or so she thought.

Then, in an unguarded moment, he'd explained that he felt the days on Earth were numbered. And looking at the way the world was, he had a point. So he'd chosen to be single, focused on staying alive and serving Daniel and Arabella and following the Rescuer. She told him she understood.

Now she'd met the Rescuer, she really did understand. Life had a new sense of urgency and fragility. Part of her still felt it was a waste, though: Micah staying single. But it did make meeting up with Lake much less complicated. Or so she hoped.

Arabella answered a knock at the door. She opened it to Lake and her husband.

Rachel stared at Lake. He stared at her. It seemed like an age since she'd last set eyes on him. He was still gorgeous though he looked a bit rough. He was wearing his tatty skater's trousers and a baggy T-shirt. There were rings under his eyes. After he looked at her, he stared at Micah. Rachel noted this.

Micah nodded politely and left the room. Two Alpha males in one small space is never a good thing, thought Rachel.

Daniel swept past Lake and embraced his wife. They went off to the back of the house to catch up with each other. This left

Rachel and Lake standing alone in the front room.

Rachel felt her heart beating fast for several seconds as they stood in silence. He was back. Her Lake was back. Was he still her Lake?

Then he giggled and said, "Wow, Rach. Your hair looks fantastic." He disarmed her with his smile. It was a broad, handsome smile that placed dimples at either side of his square jaw. Her heart fluttered and she hoped he didn't notice. She breathed out heavily, trying to mask her feelings, and shook her head.

"I made a massive mistake," he said.

"I didn't write that note," she said, almost at the same time.

"What?" they asked at the same time.

"Bind, bind, double bind!" he shouted.

"Don't be such a kid."

"But you said it at the same time!"

"Okay. What do you mean you didn't write the note?" Lake's brain caught up with her words.

"I think it was that girl," Rachel said quietly.

"Kumiko? Yes, that makes sense."

"You're an idiot."

"Yeah, I know."

"Did you two...?"

"Oh, no. I made a really big mistake, like I said. Bigger than you can imagine. But we didn't, you know, get together."

"Then what?"

"I left my job. She offered me a better one. At least, I thought it would be better. But it wasn't. It was a trap."

"What do you mean?"

"She's, like, in charge where they run things. The people in charge now. It seemed like a really good move for me. Writing for the people in charge. You know?"

"I'm listening." Rachel had her arms folded. They were now sitting on the seats. She was in a single chair. He was on a sofa. There was a coffee table between them.

"Tell me the truth now, Lake. You like her, don't you? I could tell in the pub. The Pirate's Paradise. Actually, don't tell me. It doesn't matter now. Anyway. Everything's changed."

"I'm just sorry. That's all."

"You're an idiot. A village idiot."

Lake pulled a face and nodded.

"I forgive you Lake," she breathed softly. "For whatever. I forgive you for being an idiot. I know what it is to be forgiven - of everything. And to have a fresh start - for everything."

Lake visibly relaxed.

"I thought we were finished. You and me. I got your note," he said softly.

"I didn't write it," she said sadly.

"I know that now. But I thought…"

Rachel stared hard at him. He gazed deeply into her big brown eyes. Like soft wax, her heart melted in her chest.

"I never meant to hurt you."

"For a writer, you're full of clichés," she smiled.

"All right," he sighed. "I do think about you all the time. And I miss you."

Rachel looked back at him and found herself saying, "I miss you too, Lake."

She added, "So much has changed since I last saw you. And I don't just mean my hair. There are things I've seen. Things that will blow your mind."

"I haven't a clue what you're talking about," he smiled.

"No, you don't do you?" she agreed.

"So tell me."

"Well, I met someone."

Lake raised an eyebrow. "I knew it. It's him, isn't it?" He nodded towards the back of the house to indicate Micah. "Pretty boy."

Rachel laughed. "Oh, no. It's not like that!"

Lake looked flummoxed. "What then?" he demanded.

Their conversation was interrupted by a hard, triple knock at the door. "To be continued," Lake insisted.

"Okay." Rachel got up slowly. She wondered who it was. Everyone was in the house: Daniel, Arabella, Micah and the kids, herself, Eddie and Lake. Apprehensively, she opened the door. As soon as she realised who it was, her face became radiant. Two muscular arms went around her shoulders.

"Rachel, I'm back," said Caleb Noble. "And I'd like to introduce you to my friend Serena. Believe it or not, she knew your name before I even met you."

A tanned, freckled woman with wild, wavy blonde hair stood on the doorstep. She wore a summer dress covered in small lilac flowers. Her eyes shone like green Christmas lights on a tree.

Finding her manners, Rachel said, "Please come in, both of you."

Caleb grinned at Lake Emerson, showing a line of white teeth. He had short white hair and smiling eyes and he was built like a middleweight boxer. It was just as Lake had remembered from the time he'd been held prisoner at the old house near Griffton Cliff.

"Aha," was all he could say. And, "It's you."

"Mr Emerson. Pleasure to see you again. I did tell you to wait until I came back for you, didn't I?" said Caleb.

"You certainly did." And then again, "you certainly did."

Caleb's words from last year had remained with him all this time. He became flooded with a strong memory of the presence of the Dunamis. The flow of spirit and heat and power and love. It had turned the prison where he'd been held into a place of freedom. Unbelievable freedom. Life-changing freedom. But he had pushed it to the back of his mind all this time. How could such freedom be a reality?

Caleb placed his hand on Lake's shoulder.

"Are you with us, boy?" He peered into Lake's eyes. Lake felt peace and power course through his body. It flowed out from where Caleb's hand rested. It rolled through his body like the ocean swell that flowed relentlessly towards the beach at night.

Feeling like a small child in the company of a giant, he said,

"Yes. I'm with you."

"Good for you. Come with us. We'll do you good. Now, where are the others? We need to talk to you all."

"Everyone's here. Daniel, Arabella, Dad. I'll go get them," said Rachel.

Chapter 6

Their time at Mount Makalu was at an end. The ancient Watchers, all two hundred of them with their horrific Nephilim offspring, needed to move on.

They were free from their prison beneath the mountains. There they had dwelt for millennia, punished for their rebellion. Bound until the time of imprisonment was complete. There they had waited for uncountable years in the darkness. Their hearts were abandoned, without hope. Filled only with a dark lust for violent revenge. And still they remained determined not to bow their knee to anyone. Certainly not the Creator who had subdued them. They hated him above all, and his Rescuer and their Dunamis. Their rage drove them on.

Before they left, they hit Makalu like an earthquake. Their roaring and baying polluted the air. It was deep and guttural, horrid to behold.

Under a grey and overcast sky, they razed the prehistoric mountain to the ground with furious fists and deadly fire. No longer did it boast a pyramid-shaped top. Instead it resembled a pile of dense rubble. They left Makalu Barun National Park behind in ruins. They triggered a series of huge avalanches. These rolled across the range, passing from mountain to mountain. The ground shook and great walls of snow plummeted downwards at hundreds of miles an hour. They crashed at the base of the mountains, engulfing towns and villages, streams and forests.

In the midst of this chaos, with dull eyes and smouldering contempt, Samyaza led his venomous troops. Roaring, stamping and gnashing his teeth, he took them slowly forwards.

Wild and unpredictable, some of them bounded in the opposite direction, looking for humans to terrorise. But many of the people had been obliterated by their wave of destruction. The creatures returned to the pack, angered further.

The demonic crowd took a north-westerly route to the centre of Nepal and upwards through the tops of India and Pakistan. They stayed in the hill country, surrounded by towering grey and black rock.

Samyaza wanted to tramp through the snowy peaks, enjoying his freedom and railing against the world. He desired solitude. But not the solitude of captivity. He wanted to walk under the stars and dwell amongst the mountains. He wanted to see the world he was about to inherit. And then, when he was satisfied, he would lead his army west, on to victory.

°°°°°12345°°°°°

They sought the Rescuer and spent time in the beautiful presence of his Dunamis. Lake was wowed once again, just as he had been all that time ago in the Samyaza followers' house.

The effect was completely otherworldly. He would have difficulty describing it. But if he had to, he would say something about a feeling of great love and unity with the others in the room - including Rachel. There was something about this Dunamis that seemed to knit their hearts together. He was so relieved that Rachel had forgiven him for Kumiko.

The Dunamis had further healing for Rachel and Eddie. As they bathed in the glory of the one who loved them, their affection for each other grew. The Rescuer strengthened their resolve, and filled them with hope and joy. The boys sang a quiet song of affection for the Rescuer that they had composed themselves. For Rachel, it was more wonderful than the best love song she'd ever heard.

Eddie was reminded again of his adventure with the King and his horse. It would forever be a precious time between the two of them. Rachel recalled seeing her father plummet into the lake for her to rescue. She looked at his white hair and felt closer to him than she'd ever been.

As for Daniel, Arabella and the children, this time of communing with the Dunamis put a rod of steel into them as a family. The couple had a friendship beyond words. It gave the two of them an inner beauty.

Equally, Caleb, Serena and Micah experienced a strengthening: individually and corporately. The Dunamis breathed new life into them and they felt stronger for it: better equipped for what lay ahead.

Their time together in the presence of the Rescuer came to a gentle end. Each of them felt their hearts glowing. An atmosphere of gentleness and respect filled the air.

"We are ready," Caleb declared. They sat in a loose circle, on sofas and dining chairs with Caleb at the head. The boys sat on the floor. Eddie had set a couple of bowls of crisps on the table but these were largely untouched. It was only Rory who went up from time to time to swipe a crisp for himself or his brother. They crunched them quietly.

"First things first. I'd formally like to introduce my wife and travelling companion to you."

A loud murmur rippled through the room and Serena smiled and blushed, showing off a sparkling wedding ring. The boys clapped.

"Yeah, I know. Blame the angels. They married us."

"It's true! It's true," said Serena. "They brought Caleb and me together separately in the mezzanine and a troop of Warrior Angels stood to attention in the valley while Mattatron, one of the lead angels, married us in the sight of the King. I still haven't come down from the experience."

Caleb paused, smiled and forged ahead with his introductions, refusing to be drawn into the conversation. "Serena, this is my good friend Daniel. That's his wife Arabella, and Rory and Cameron. Watch out for Rory's jokes. Cameron will tell you everything about the world and how it works." The boys giggled, delighted that they got a proper introduction.

"Hi folks. Good to know you all," said Serena with a grin. She had a soft American accent. Rachel took to her instantly.

Caleb continued, "This is, of course, Rachel."

"Rachel, it's such a pleasure to meet you in real life. Caleb and the Dunamis told me so much about you. And what you've had to go through."

"And this is Eddie, and Micah."

Serena smiled at them.

Then Caleb moved straight on to business. "Daniel, Eddie, Rachel, tell me what you know. How is this city faring in the grip of the enemy?"

Daniel shook his head. "Not good. Lake tells me the enemy has destroyed buildings, communities and lives. They're blaming us, as you'd expect. The people are living in fear. People are disappearing. No one knows what the future holds. It's classic Samyaza."

Caleb nodded in agreement.

"I managed to get into my house. This guy was there, in my study." Daniel nodded towards Lake.

"Can we trust him?" asked Micah.

Rachel looked offended. "Yes, Micah. We can trust him. He may be an idiot, agreeing to take a job with the enemy. But we can trust him."

"Okay," said Caleb. "We know the enemy is on his way. He is in possession of his body and has his Nephilim with him."

"That sounds bad," Lake noted. He shuffled in his seat.

"Word is they're travelling by foot and will take many days to arrive. They are positioning Grigori and Nephilim around the world in strategic places."

"They're coming here? To Griffton?" asked Lake.

"Griffton seems to be their epicentre of choice," said Caleb.

"They are coming from the mountains in Nepal where the Initiation occurred. My guess is they will come through Eastern Europe and across the western nations."

"Yikes," said Lake. "Is there any stopping them? Can anyone stop them?"

"Yes. We will stop them," said Rory confidently. Lake did a double take. He stared at Rory, impressed by his youthful confidence.

"Yes, we will." Caleb echoed. "We believe the time is now upon us to activate the Protectors. This is what a messenger told us when we were in New York."

"A messenger?" asked Lake.

"An angel. From the Creator and his Rescuer."

Lake didn't know what to say.

"Don't worry, Lake. You will see them for yourself before long," Caleb said. "Serena now knows the locations for all three Protectors: of land, sea and air. We must go to them and do what the Dunamis prompts us to do."

"And what is that?" Daniel enquired.

"We don't know yet."

"And are we going to split up or stick together?"

"To go as fast as we can we must travel in three groups."

"How far are we going?" asked Rachel.

"Far. Very far. But we can cover the distance more quickly by going through the mezzanine."

Arabella shuddered. Eddie grinned. Rachel exchanged glances with Micah. Lake looked left out.

"Now, are you ready for your groups and locations?"

"I think so," said Rachel, "But how are we going to know how to get there or what to do once we're there? What exactly are the Protectors? How do we activate them?"

"So many questions," said Serena softly. She smiled sweetly to Rachel. "This is how I live. Welcome to my life. The Dunamis will lead us, and he will tell us what we need when we need it. It means we stay fully reliant on him."

"And that's okay is it?" snapped Lake. He felt like he was trying to stay afloat on the top of a deep, black ocean.

"Yes. That's okay," said Caleb, turning his face to him. "We are servants of the Highest. We're in the safest place we can be."

"So, what are our groups?" asked Daniel. "I need to be with Bella and the kids."

"Don't worry," Caleb reassured him. "Daniel, Arabella, Rory and Cameron. We'd like you to activate the Sea Protector. You will find it on a Pacific island. It's near Hawaii."

Arabella looked pleased.

"Rachel, Eddie, Lake, you're Bhutan. The mountains. That's the Air Protector."

"Mountains," said Rachel. She shivered.

"And myself, Serena and Micah are going to Tanzania to a natural crater in the earth. There we will look for the Land Protector. And we will activate it."

Caleb sat back in his chair. He ran the palm of his hand over his closely-cut white hair and looked thoughtful. Rachel was encouraged by the change in him since his rescue in the caves of the mezzanine when he'd lost all hope. Sitting before them was a new man – renewed and focused.

He spoke softly but firmly. "If anyone is unclear on why we are doing this, we must fight Samyaza, his Grigori and their Nephilim to the death. They are a ruthless and relentless enemy. They will not stop until the whole world is under their control. And they don't care if man lives or dies. I know this first hand. They killed my friends," he cried out. "They killed Eli and Anton," Caleb yelped. He shook his head, and Serena put her hand on his shoulder.

Then he pulled himself together and continued. "So, be strong and very courageous. But be wary; be watchful. Our adversary is prowling around like a roaring lion looking for someone to devour. Stand firm against him, and be strong. The enemy is a defeated foe and his destiny is ultimately to lose. The Rescuer is by your side and his Dunamis is with you. When things get hard, lean on him. I want you to know I have seen the angel armies standing prepared in the valleys of the mezzanine. They are ready to take ground as we take ground. So, keep fighting. Never give up. And let's meet up and celebrate in the world to come, when the work is done. Are you with me?"

"We are," said Eddie and Daniel together.

"Are you all with me?"

"We are!" said everyone together. This time, Eddie and Daniel's voices were joined with everyone in the room, including the children. Including Lake.

Rachel turned to him and gave him her special smile.

"Pack a bag. Travel light. We leave in one hour. The enemy's on the move," said Caleb.

Chapter 7

Arabella was trying to get her head around the practicalities of packing.

Regarding her children she said: "It sounds like it's going to be hot where we're going. So, boys, you don't need much. It's a good job I washed your clothes yesterday. By the way, thanks awfully for the spare T-shirts, Rachel."

Rachel thought Arabella looked stunning herself. She wore a pale pink tailored shirt and jacket with ankle boots and jeans. She carried an extra T-shirt and sandals in her bag.

"You look great, boys." Rachel admired the children dressed in black rock-band T-shirts that were too large for them. They looked very handsome. Rory peered through his long fringe with intense brown eyes. The boys still had their rucksacks with them from their house. They contained all of their essential items. Amazingly, they hadn't complained about having to leave all their toys and tech at home.

As for Rachel, she was used to being away from home now and living off the bare minimum. She placed into her pack her phone, toothbrush and toothpaste, eyeliner and a spare change of clothes. Since she was going to the mountains, she found her warmest coat and gloves and put these in a separate bag.

They distributed the food between all of them. Rachel didn't feel hungry now and knew she wouldn't in the mezzanine. That was a place where your appetite shrank, except if you were with the Rescuer.

Lake came into the front room and started fidgeting around. He changed into his warmest clothes: a thick cotton checked shirt, coupled with his combat trousers. There was a dark coat over his arm.

"So, where are we going again?"

Rachel said patiently, "It's a place that you can get to from Griffton Cliff. But it's not part of Griffton. You'll see, Lake. They call it the mezzanine world."

"And if I go there, my hair might turn white?"

Rachel stared at him with a smirk. "There is a possibility that your hair will turn white, Lake. Yes."

"Okay. So are going up to the cliff?"

"Yes, Lake. We're going up to the cliff."

"Okay."

By now, Daniel, Micah, Serena and Eddie had come into the front room. It was feeling distinctly crowded with all of them and their luggage.

The excitement was almost tangible. They were going on the adventure of their lives. Nobody knew exactly where they were going. No one had a clue how things would end up or if they would ever return to Griffton. They knew the odds were stacked against them. But they also knew they had no choice. The Protectors needed to be activated, whatever that meant. Somehow they were unable to activate themselves. And they were the only ones who could do it.

"I've arranged for three cabs to come and pick us up," explained Daniel. "They'll be here soon. We'll go in convoy up to Griffton Cliff. Then we'll go through to the other side together."

"The other side? You mean the mezzanine?" Lake asked dubiously.

"You're gonna love it, man," Caleb grinned at him.

°°°°°12345°°°°°

They walked the distance from Lower Ledge Crossing to the top of the cliff. It was a relatively steep climb but everyone was buoyed by the adventure. The boys even found the energy to race ahead. They all made the summit easily.

It was evening and the view of the city was spectacular. The human eye could pick out tiny details from the buildings and streets with ease, the air was so clear. You could even see the waves down at the foot of the city, lit by the last few hours of sunlight.

"That's my Griffton," said Lake. He closed his eyes and felt the evening breeze on his face. "It's still beautiful despite what's happened."

"We used to come up here, didn't we?" Rachel commented, quietly.

"Yeah."

"You, me and your terrible jokes."

"Easy there."

The top of the cliff was quiet, calm and empty. The long grass rippled gently along the northern slope. It looked like a field of tiny creatures racing each other, back and forth. There were a few birds that hopped along the wild shrubs and trees that dotted the dusty cliff path. They flew out and returned again, grey boomerangs, spinning out and in.

"So, how do we get to this place? This mezzanine?"

"You see that stone head over there?" Rachel asked.

"Yes, of course."

"That's kind of like the door."

"I don't see any handle."

"Well, that's the door, Lake." Rachel beamed. "You'll never believe it."

"Okay, I'll take your word for it." He furrowed his brow and walked towards the stone head which stood ten feet tall. It had deep-set eyes and a vacant, yet somehow unsettling expression. Its cheeks looked closely shaved, smooth and grey.

"Seen it before?" Daniel asked.

"I came up to see it after it appeared," said Lake. "I was curious, you know. But I didn't touch it. I heard the stories."

"Well, you need to touch it now."

"Is it safe?"

"It depends what you mean by safe," said Caleb, laughing.

"Are we going to hang around here all day chatting?" Eddie boomed. "Come on." He set his will and marched towards the head. He tramped the long grass as he went. Lake's eyes widened as the large figure of Eddie dissolved into the stony surface, like a sugar cube dropped into a mug of hot tea.

Lake gasped and then said, "I get it. A doorway."

The others pushed past him and went through, passing from Griffton into another world.

"It's okay," said Rachel. "Go through - and don't get left behind!" She departed his side and made her way into the mezzanine.

"Yes, come along, Lake. But get ready. You never know what you might meet on the other side," said Caleb as he ran through.

On his own now, Lake stood and scratched the back of his head. He took one last look at Griffton city and picked up his stuff.

"So long, Griffton. Been nice knowing ya!" he called as he moved through the portal.

°°°°°°12345°°°°°°

Rachel was relieved to find they had gone through to the same place as last time. She looked up at the crazy purple sky. It was shot through with pink swirls: wispy strands of candy floss.

She found herself surrounded again by massive mountains made from dark red rocks. She saw the hanging trees and boulders, defying nature; defying logic. This time the air was filled with static. Grey dots flickered above their heads, overlaying the forest of rocks and trees. It was as though an ancient movie was being projected into the space above them.

Despite the strangeness, Rachel felt like she was home. She was fonder of this place than she should be. After all, the mezzanine had attempted to kill her on a number of occasions.

Lake was by her side looking confused and shocked. She must have looked like that herself when she first came through. She remembered jumping at every movement and new sight. Slowly and apprehensively Lake put one foot in front of the other. All the while he repeated to himself: "This isn't real. This place isn't real."

The Harcourt family were also huddled together, acclimatising themselves to the mezzanine world again. Daniel looked protective, with his arms around as many family members as he could reach, including Micah.

Only Caleb and Serena were confident, standing tall. They looked slowly around them, scanning the horizon for friends or foes.

Before long, Caleb called everyone together in order to regroup. They positioned themselves by some dark boulders which afforded them protective cover. The boys sat down by their feet.

Caleb explained, "The last time we came here, we went through that valley in front of us and towards a set of caves a long way off. That's where my friends died at the hands of the shape shifter. Be on the lookout for him. He's a dangerous enemy and he lives over there." He pointed across the basin.

"When we get to the caves, we'll split up and go in three separate directions to find the portals that will take us to our destinations. I'll brief you all closer to the time. Mainly because that's all Serena and I know at present!"

Nobody had any questions so they set off across the open ground, ridged by hills on either side. They left the stone statue behind them.

°°°°°*12345*°°°°°

As they walked, the children ran in circles around the adults, whooping and hollering with joy. They bounded high into the air, imagining they were spacemen. Their hearts reflected the excitement of the landscape with its crazy edges and angles. Arabella frequently called out for them to be careful as she spotted a dangerous root or crack in the ground.

Daniel put his arm around Arabella and walked by her side. He gently encouraged her to leave the children to enjoy their adventure. If they took a tumble, then they would deal with it, he said.

Rachel smiled, finding herself able to take in this part of the mezzanine world properly – unlike last time. When she first arrived here, she was so scared that she hadn't taken the opportunity to enjoy the beautiful views. Instead, it had chilled her to the bone. But this world was spectacular and worth drinking in.

Eddie concurred. He seemed delighted to be back in the mezzanine. Hungry for adventure, he grinned in an unhinged way. He stared all around him. Sometimes he spun three hundred and sixty degrees, pulling everything in through his eyes. From the red moon above down to the ground beneath them with its holes and gaps that fell away to blackness below. He took it all in.

As they walked forwards it dawned on Lake that the place was, in fact, real. His brain started to adjust to this fact. But it took a while. He caught himself relaxing and then feeling the adrenalin rush of fear. He couldn't feel anything, though his brain kept trying to fill in for the absent sensations. His senses were messed up, and this was disorientating.

Soon, he realised that time was passing as it does in the real world. Moment by moment. The scenery remained constant as they walked by. The sky was relatively still, though the colours were surreal. But it didn't shift and change as it does in a dream.

On the other hand, he couldn't feel very much: heat, cold, wind or even the ground beneath his feet. In truth, he felt like he was floating on air. But he was also aware he was with other people and could hear their conversation and this felt real.

His mind started to calm down. He enjoyed the view across the valley. There were scrubby bushes and spiky trees, though they grew sideways which was baffling. There were also some unusual combinations of colour: purples and yellows; blacks and reds. The pebbles and rocks spun slowly, dangling in mid-air. The place held equal measures of wonder and horror for him.

They kept walking. Floating.

°°°°°*12345*°°°°°

Daniel and Arabella held the boys' hands as they crossed the gappy crazy-paving that was the valley floor. Every so often somebody stepped awkwardly or missed their footing. It was hard to walk when you couldn't feel your feet, particularly for the boys. There were gasps as people realised again that beneath them was nothing: just a sheer drop into the chasm below.

"So," said Lake, "you've been here before, Rachel?"

"Yes, I spent some time here. It's a beautiful place, Lake. But there are things we need to be wary of. There's a man who changes his shape: a shape shifter. Caleb mentioned him. He can look like people that you know. He's called Zaelaza – Zed. And he has a pale son who can turn himself into a hundred copies. Maybe more. It's way creepy."

"Sounds like a horror movie."

"Well, they're real enough. And they're very dangerous. We need to be careful if we bump into them. And we just need to trust the Dunamis to keep us safe."

Lake nodded seriously.

"There are also big black creatures that have wings and fangs."

"Horror movie," said Lake.

"They look like bats and they have leather all over them and they stink. You don't want to get stuck with one of them either. Oh, and there might be big cats as well."

"Cats?"

"You know, cheetahs and panthers and stuff."

"Not again! This place is starting to freak me out," said Lake.

"On the good side, there are angels here."

"You are kidding me?"

61

"They protect us and are ready to help. I met one and they are, like, really huge."

"Okay," said Lake. "Anything else I need to know?"

"Well, the Rescuer is also here and if you meet him it will change your life. For definite."

"Anything else?"

"There's a place I love called Rachel's Pool and it's probably not really called Rachel's Pool, but that's what we call it."

"We?"

"Me and the Rescuer."

"Okay."

"And it's got warm water and a waterfall that runs down. I hope we get to go past it so I can show you. It's a really good place. Beautiful. And you know that feeling we get when we meet the Dunamis together?"

"Yes," he said, reluctantly.

"Well, the water feels like that. It's hard to explain it."

"You're doing a pretty good job."

"It's through this valley and down a cliff, I think. But hopefully we won't have to fall down and bounce off all the rocks like I did last time. And land in a big lake."

"I have no idea what you're talking about."

"It doesn't matter. So, tell me what's been happening in Griffton."

"Rachel, it was terrible. Absolutely horrific. These bombs went off, like I said. I was working at the time, so I got to cover them for the paper. Spike made an emergency news room, round the clock. All hands on deck. It was such a waste of life though. Awful really."

He continued, "I went to the police station and saw what they'd done. The place was gutted. It was just so sad. There was rubble everywhere and glass. And the smell. It was too much. And I thought my dad was dead. But he was okay. He works near the government building, you know. The one that was bombed as well. I thought it was a good idea to go and work with the people who are protecting us. I thought they were the good guys. I got it wrong."

Lake was silent for a while and they carried on walking.

"And Kumi wasn't the person I thought she was. She's a liar. And she seems to enjoy what they're doing. She's kind of in charge. Or high up, anyway, even though she's our age! I know they're the ones behind the bombing. I know it now. I didn't then."

Rachel nodded kindly.

"And they had me writing stuff. Lies about what they're doing. Protecting everyone and running law and order. And trying to hunt down the followers of the Dunamis and the Rescuer. But like I say, now I know it's all lies. So I was living in the big house, Daniel's house. Lytescote Manor. And they kept me prisoner there and wouldn't let me leave. And she kept shouting at me about my writing and said it wasn't any good. She was really cruel, Rach. But I know I'm a good writer. I've had front-page stories, haven't I? So that's it really. I haven't seen my parents yet. I haven't seen my friends. I don't know how they are."

He stared at the ground for a while. Rachel wanted to take his hand, but didn't.

"How about you?"

"Well, like I said. I spent some time here and I met the Rescuer. Oh, Lake he's wonderful. He's like no one else. He made me new. He makes everything new. He's the reason that we live. He made me come alive." She realised she was almost singing the words.

"It sounds a bit crazy to me. I don't really understand what you're saying, though I can hear the words," said Lake.

"Oh, that's okay. Maybe you'll meet him face to face. Him and his great big white horse."

Lake made his eyes big and laughed.

"All right, girl. Let's see."

Chapter 8

It was a long walk. Senses and sensations were returning to the group, with the boys reporting every development.

"Breeze on my face!" exclaimed Cameron.

"I can feel the ground!" shouted Rory. "Ouch! Sharp rocks."

"Smelly lava," said Cameron, peering into a crack.

"Hungry yet?"

"No, not me," said Rory.

"Nor me."

They travelled parallel to a jagged line of black mountains, over craggy rocks, loose shingle and shiny stones. Red flowers bloomed sporadically, rooted into the ground between the rocks. They had thin stems that glistened and they smelled of nectarines. Although the group had to watch their step lest they trip over the gaps, they relaxed a little and chatted. They could see for miles around and there was no apparent sign of danger.

Rachel had the opportunity to talk to Caleb. She really enjoyed listening to him. He was lively and interesting. His voice was full of expression and warmth.

"I used to be a pilot, you know."

"Yes, I heard," she said, nodding for him to continue.

"I flew long haul all over the world. I really enjoyed it. It was a fantastic job to have. Sometimes I flew out to places in America – New York or Houston. Other times it was the Middle East or Africa. I'd fly all the way there and have one or maybe two days' turnaround and come back again. But I didn't mind that the stay was so short. It meant I got to see the world and I had friends all over the place. People I could have coffee with and just fall right back into a good friendship. Have you ever flown?"

"No, not me. I'm a Griffton girl. I've never really been out of Griffton, except London and Solihull, and a couple of other places. Polcombe down the road," she laughed.

"And the mezzanine?"

"Oh yeah. Here," she smiled. "You don't need a passport for this place. Anyway, tell me more."

"All right. The way it worked was I'd maybe fly for a shift. There were three pilots rotating. I'd have three hours of rest on the plane when I wasn't in the cockpit. So, I'd sit in First Class which is special: a real treat. Lots of leg-room and great service. I'd have a glass of champagne and some olives and watch a movie or two. It was a wonderful job. My body clock got a bit messed up but that was okay. I didn't mind leaving for the airport late at night or very early in the morning. It was all part of the job. You get used to it."

They had reached the end of the valley and were starting to climb. Rachel remembered this part of the journey. She touched a tall rock which thrust its nose high into the air. She still couldn't feel any sensation in her hands or feet. Consequently, she floated through this strange land like a bubble.

Caleb kept talking and Rachel enjoyed his rich voice. "I had a wife, you know. She was called Rosemary. But she died."

"Sorry."

"Thank you. It was really hard. But the Rescuer was always there for me. He showed me the bigger picture that there is more to life than this one, if you know what I mean?"

"Yes, I'm getting the idea," said Rachel.

"There's so much more even in this life that we could get to know. Peace beyond our dreams. A joy that fills your heart to bursting, even when things get difficult. Love beyond measure. Freedom. True freedom. Ours for the taking."

"I'm learning these things slowly," said Rachel.

"And then there's the wonder of knowing the King and his presence and hearing him through his Dunamis. And he's good and he loves us."

"Have you met him too?"

"Yes. Do you remember when the angel Mattatron brought me back to you outside the caves?"

"Yes I do. Aha, he turned your hair white then, didn't he? Just like mine. I did wonder about that."

"Yes. I met him when I most needed to. When I doubted his love the most, he brought me to him. The angels brought me to him. Imagine that. Caleb Noble, widower. Traveller. Strong-willed ox that I am. And he cares for me."

"I hope we bump into him here," whispered Rachel.

"Do you know what? Whether we do or not, it doesn't matter," said Caleb. "He is with us now."

Rachel nodded. They were ahead of the others so they halted to allow them to catch up. The dark green oval-shaped valley lay behind them, stretching back to the stone head which was no longer visible. They could pick out spatters of red here and there: tall flowers that rose up on long stems amidst the dark rocks and stones.

"So how did you and Serena meet?" asked Rachel.

"Well that's a funny thing. It was because of you. I was travelling in Nepal. In the mountains. Hiking. It was when the Initiation happened. You remember."

"How could I forget?"

"Well, I knew I had to go to Indonesia, to the island of Bali. That's what the Dunamis had spoken. So, he took me to meet her by the sea. Serena. And we ate coconut fish and she had a flower in her hair and a little summer dress and I fell in love with her."

He gazed at Serena in the distance as she laughed with Arabella. His eyes were soft and a smile played about his lips. "I never thought there would be anyone after Rosemary. But I was wrong," he murmured. "And the Rescuer knows our hearts and he knows what we need. So he put us together, and he joined our hearts together. The end."

"Or should that be 'the beginning'? That is so romantic. And she's lovely. So beautiful. Inside and out."

"Yes she is," agreed Caleb. "And kind. And gentle. Everything a rough old bear like me needs. Well, like I said, it was because of you. And she knew you were the first of the five and that the Rescuer had made you special, although he loves everyone equally." He looked her in the face.

"How am I special?"

"Oh, I think you know that," said Caleb.

"Not really."

"Well, it's not for me to say then," Caleb answered. His mouth became a wide line: a smile particular to Caleb Noble.

"So I met her again in New York and we stood with an angel and looked over New York from above Times Square. He told us about the Protectors and it was like our hearts melted together there and then and became one. Like when you join two pipes together with liquid solder. Now I am hers and she is mine. We got married, you know."

"Yes, you said at the house: congratulations!"

"After you went through the stone head and returned back to Griffton, Mattatron kept me behind and made me wait. I didn't know what I was waiting for. I thought it was the King. But no. It was Serena. I might be the only dude in history who gets to be married by the angelic host."

"Amazing! That is so beautiful."

The others caught up. Before they regrouped, Rachel enquired of Caleb, "Is it going to get hard do you think? What we have to do. Will it get tough? Like what happened with the Malkin?" Rachel felt as though she was forcing herself to look at something she'd rather not. Like a gross bug or fungus on a tree.

"Yes, I believe it is. The enemy will throw everything he can at us to stop us activating the Protectors. But you know that the Dunamis is with you. So keep smiling!"

They didn't go upwards towards Zed's house, although they did glimpse the dark and foreboding structure that sat brooding on the black obsidian plateau. Instead, Serena followed the Dunamis to lead them a different way. Their path snaked downwards, quite steeply at times, into another valley. Rachel was relieved to avoid the horrible Zed.

The path curved around and around until they started to see a wall of rock rising skywards. Rachel guessed that the lake was inside that walled area, along with the forest and Rachel's Pool. And so they descended under the purple sky, down into the unknown.

Lake gazed up at the ridges of brown and red. "How long do you think this place has been around?" he asked.

"I don't really know," said Rachel.

They asked Caleb and Serena who also had no idea.

Caleb speculated, "It could have been around longer than the Earth, or perhaps as long as it has existed."

"Are we even on the Earth?," asked Eddie. "Could the portal have sent us to the Moon or Mars? If you think about it, there are geological features here that defy the laws of physics. Things like gravity or inertia. I reckon the creatures who live here predate humans."

There was so much they didn't know about this world or their own, Rachel concluded.

°°°°°°*12345*°°°°°°

Kyrgyzstan connects with Kazakhstan to the north, Uzbekistan to the west and Tajikistan to the south. China is to the east.

Majestic peaks line the border and tower above the usually serene rural landscape. But not today. Like a tornado, the Grigori and their Nephilim tore through the border, leaving carnage in their wake. In an instant, they transformed a calm July morning into the darkest night.

Imagine a blade of a mower a mile wide cutting through a landscape at two hundred miles an hour. That was the devastation reaped by the dark menace rampaging across the eastern border of the J-shaped country. Bent on destruction and with a hatred for humans in their twisted hearts, the enemy wrought their revenge on the created beings.

As for the ancient villages in the valley: all was rubble. A tiny handful of survivors clawed and picked through the debris with their bare hands, listening out for signs of life. They were growing increasingly rare. Many were dead or dying, lacerated by the passing evil. Bodies were torn and mangled. All the children from a small elementary school were missing. Dead camels and goats littered the green countryside as the pale mountains gazed down impassively.

The remains of a rich man's house lay in a heap. A grey-white toilet was all that was left of his impressive building, once the envy of his neighbours. Except for the rounded bowl, everything was debris and rubble and the man lay buried beneath it all, the toilet acting as his tombstone.

A solitary car lay on its roof. It was as though a formidable force had scooped it up and hurled it onto its back. This wasn't far from the truth. Nothing was as it had been. The land now had a long gash through it that stretched for miles. Veins of destruction tore off in different directions as the enemy peeled away to target cities across the globe. There, they would position a Grigori to oversee the nation, and a cluster of Nephilim to ravage and spoil it.

Moving slowly, the destructive convoy continued on their leisurely journey towards Western Europe, roaring at the clouds, screaming at the sky.

°°°°°*12345*°°°°°

They found Rachel's Pool. Only, it was no longer recognisable as the place she had enjoyed so much. The waterfall still thundered down the rocks and gushed into the canyon. But the rocky bowl had been cloven from the bottom to the top. It was broken down and desecrated. Huge chunks of curved grey rock lay on the forest floor. The force required to smash it up must have been considerable. Rachel couldn't stop crying. Her pool was beyond repair.

Lake held her in his arms, trying in vain to comfort her. He enjoyed holding her and nestling his face in her hair. Unfortunately, the words he chose were inappropriate. "Don't cry. It's only a pile of rocks and a waterfall. It's okay."

"You don't get it," she sobbed. "You don't understand. That was my pool. Rachel's Pool. And they've broken it. It was my secret place. The place I met him. The water was special."

She sank down to the ground, with Lake still holding her, and hugged her knees. Her bottom sat in a pool of water and Lake knelt by her side. The others stood off at a distance, resting, chatting, and looking over quizzically from time to time. Rachel's father looked concerned but left Lake to look after her.

Eventually, her sobs gave way to deep sighs and she started to feel the Dunamis swell inside her. Lake perceived her body growing less rigid and he loosened his embrace. She felt the presence of the Dunamis filling her chest, making her calm. She enjoyed the feeling and relaxed, waiting unhurriedly. The sound of the waterfall filled her mind. Then she shut her eyes and the King spoke to her heart.

"Rest and relax, Rachel. The enemy meant harm for this place. Your place. And he meant harm for you. But do not be sad and do not be anxious. Rachel's Pool is not a place. Rachel's Pool is in your heart. And there you will find me. I am in you and you are in me, and we are in the one who made it all: the Creator. So take heart and do not grieve. Rachel's Pool is not a place. Rachel's Pool is in your heart."

Rachel looked up at Lake. He really was handsome. And clueless. And she loved him.

"It's okay. I'm fine now. Let's go," she said.

He furrowed his brow. "Really?"

"It's cool. It would have been nice to swim about in the pool but it's gone now and that's okay. Help me up. Let's go."

°°°°°*12345*°°°°°

Night was falling in the mezzanine. The red sun sank beneath the tree-line, leaving a spectacular plum coloured sky that darkened by the second. The group huddled together. They didn't feel cold, but rather, exposed to the elements and whatever was lurking out there.

They decided to hunker down near the wall of the canyon, rather than venture out further. Besides, it was difficult to see very far, even though there was still some light from the night sky. No one was hungry but everyone seemed tired now. The kids wanted to curl up and sleep, so they covered them in coats and formed a protective circle around them. The ground was soft and dry.

Then Rachel heard an unfamiliar sound. It was a low baying in the distance, coming from in front of them, in the direction they were travelling. It was a cross between a cry of pain and a menacing, wolfish howl.

She sat up straight. "Did you hear that?" Her heart started to pound. "Any ideas, guys?"

Caleb hushed her. He listened intently. Crouched low to the ground, he stared into the darkness.

The howl came again, racing through the mezzanine like a disembodied ghost.

Chapter 9

Caleb stood up tall and declared in a strong voice, "We are not intimidated. We are bold and courageous. Our Rescuer is with us. Nothing can touch us. Nothing that the Rescuer does not allow."

The howl came back again from the far distance. It was louder and angrier than before. It was joined by other voices, other noises. A pack of wild creatures on the hunt. The Harcourt kids huddled together next to Lake, who, until the howling began, had been making them giggle. Rachel felt her skin bristle.

Caleb roared, "We are not intimidated. We are bold and courageous. If you want us, come and get us. If not, then be silent."

Rachel felt the Dunamis strengthen her frame. Her fear started to dissipate and she sat up taller, her back against the rocks. She remembered her weapons again. Her weapons against the enemy's attack were joyful laughter and faith. Part of her remembered that these weapons had not worked against the Malkin. She had tried to muster her arms but it hadn't worked. The thought was like an abscessed tooth, aching in her jaw.

But as she reflected on Caleb's words, her resolve returned. He was right. She knew that the Dunamis was in her, and that her Rescuer loved her. He would ultimately protect her, or strengthen her through whatever difficulties she faced.

She stood up alongside Caleb in the darkness, under the eerie glow of the dark red sky. The shapes of massive trees lay ahead, monstrous in the darkness.

Then she realised it wasn't just her and Caleb. No, she definitely wasn't alone, and neither was he. Daniel, Micah and Eddie were standing with them to the right. Arabella and Serena were upright to the left, legs apart, ready for action. They were like a fortress standing against the howling wind and rain. Together they were a wall of warriors: a wall of living stones, united and ready to withstand the fiercest attack. The enemy could try his best. They were ready.

Only Lake remained seated with the kids, and that was okay. He didn't yet know the power of the Rescuer and his Dunamis. He didn't know the one who held sway over life and death, even over the forces of darkness and evil that raise their proud heads against all that is good in this world.

But eventually even he stood up and joined Rachel's side. She imagined it was because he finally realised it was what he was meant to do. But it didn't matter. He was standing by her side and that was what counted. This time, she did take his hand and held it firmly: her little hand in his.

"Can you see anything?" asked Lake.

"No. They're not coming tonight," said Caleb decidedly. "They wouldn't dare. But if they do decide to come over here, we'll be ready."

"So what should we do?" asked Rachel.

"We stay put until sun-up. Rest and try to get some sleep. Or whatever passes as sleep in this place. We'll take shifts. Serena – are you happy to watch with me for the first third of the night?"

She nodded.

"I'm not sleepy. I'll join you," said Rachel.

"Good. Daniel, Arabella, you take second shift. Micah, Eddie, Lake, third. We'll move on at first sight of daylight."

As they waited and watched through the night, Caleb led his small team in a time of communing with the Dunamis. They enjoyed sweet moments in his presence that turned into sweet hours, confident they were protected.

Rachel felt that unseen angels stood in a ring around them, singing with them and keeping their spirits up.

When it came to the handover, Caleb advised the others to do the same. And so they did, mindful of the Rescuer's great love for them. Rachel was buzzing so much that she decided to sit through the second watch as well. But by the time it got to the early hours of the mezzanine night, she was in a deep and dreamless sleep.

°°°°°*12345*°°°°°

Apart from the intermittent howling, the night passed without event. At daybreak, the group gathered their packs and coats and filed out, two by two, down into the valley.

The travellers took note of the interesting flora that grew out of the rocky ground. The children particularly liked an unusual rainbow-coloured growth that poked out like long straws. Firm and hard to the touch, this plant seemed to display a range of colours. They changed and shifted depending on the angle at which they looked at it. There were also some very sharp and spiky explosions reminiscent of sea urchins, in dark reds and purples. The sky above could have given birth to these creations as they shared similar hues.

And then there were the bubble creatures the boys so enjoyed last time they were in the mezzanine. These were tiny frogs that floated around randomly. Rory caught one on his palm, excited that the sphere didn't burst but held firm instead.

Both Rory and Cameron peered into the bubble, scrutinising the alien being inside. The dark miniature frog regarded them coolly through lidless eyes. Then the bubble floated off, without any warning. The boys agreed that the bubble was part of the frog's body, though Rory secretly held that it was like his spaceship.

Apart from these round things, they didn't spot many other animals. There was a suggestion of birds in the sky, the dark blue pterodactyl creatures that Rachel spied during her last adventure. But these flew very high up. They were hard to see clearly against the magenta sky, with its web of rocks hanging beneath. It left you with an impression of movement: like the menacing outline of a school of sharks deep beneath the surface of the sea. Black shapes circling.

Rachel was relieved that there was no sign of the cheetah she saw last time. It had appeared in the trees and tracked her as she travelled. She would be ready for it this time. However, instead of feeling apprehensive, she had fond memories of how it rolled over when she laughed. It's funny how a shift in perspective can change things, she thought.

Soon, the hard, rocky ground gave way to thick forest. Clusters of coal black trees were rooted firmly into the ground. Rachel thought the place looked familiar, though perhaps she'd entered the forest higher up last time. This was because the ground was flatter here and led straight into the forest rather than snaking downhill.

Everybody gazed in wonder at the tall black trees, lost in their immensity. Somebody talked about the massive trees you find in Canada, Redwoods and Red Creek firs which grow as tall as skyscrapers and as wide as living rooms. Just like those trees, these black ones soared like muscular sentinels.

"They must have been alive for thousands of years," commented Eddie.

"You can build a house in that one," yelled Cameron.

"A tree house!" said Rory. "Tree-house, get it?"

The boys peered up into the sky to see if they could see the tops of them, spying the umbrella branches many feet above their heads. They really wanted to climb them but couldn't find any handholds. Arabella was keen for them not to attempt it and told them so. It wasn't the climbing that bothered her but rather a potential fall from a great height.

As they walked through the forest they felt a few drops of rain start to fall on their heads. The large, warm drops were a prelude to a downpour of epic proportions. When the flood came, it was as though the magenta sky had opened up and dumped warm water on them.

This freakish weather was unexpected and made Eddie laugh out loud, wondering at this crazy place. They stood, drenched from their hair down to their feet, screaming, laughing and groaning.

They carried on walking, treading through bracken and ground that was becoming softer by the minute. The rain fell less heavily now. Their shoes became muddy and rivulets of water ran across the ground. Rory and Cameron enjoyed squelching and leaping into the puddles.

Wandering slowly, and enjoying the sensation of the droplets on their skin, the group realised again that they had now fully acclimatised to the mezzanine. They had got all of their senses back.

They enjoyed the feeling of the ground beneath their feet and the warm water on their faces. Serena grinned at Caleb, wet, strawberry blonde strands of hair in her eyes.

As quickly as it had started, the rain stopped. They squelched through pools of water and small streams ran across the floor of the woods. The trees spattered them with water from above, as leaves overflowed with their nectar. But the droplets felt cooler, stripped of their warmth by their long journey from the high canopy above. They passed through the thick woods.

Eddie and Rachel finally got to talk. Rachel had always made it a habit to avoid deep conversation with her father. But she decided to take the opportunity to see how he was and what he was thinking. And so she asked him, "Hey Dad. What do you make of the mezzanine?"

"The thing I love about this place," said Eddie animatedly, "is that there is very little that is man-made. It's like the comic books I used to read when I was a kid. We used to have these magazines about mysterious science fiction places. Their pages were filled with new worlds to explore that just opened up in my head. And they had pictures and cartoons as well as stories."

"I remember you telling me about them a long time ago," murmured Rachel. She smiled.

"I might even have a couple of them in the attic. Anyway, this place reminds me of some of those worlds. Of course, there is some stuff that must have been made by hand," Eddie continued. "The last time I came here I found a house."

"Was it made of wood? On a black rock?"

"Yeah, that's it."

"Zed's house back there? Have you been inside?" Rachel asked with a shiver.

"It was when I first came into the mezzanine. That's where I went. I walked through the valley and found it."

"Me too. He drugged me, you know," said Rachel quietly.

"Yes, I gathered."

"And those horrible boys chased me to the edge of the cliff. And I fell."

"Yeah, me too. Only they pushed me off."

"He's a bad man. A monster."

They walked in silence for a while.

"It's a very strange place," Eddie concluded.

"I know we don't talk about it much," said Rachel. "But I do miss her, you know."

Eddie fixed his eyes on the horizon and said, "So do I."

He turned to look at Rachel. "But I had a chat with the Rescuer, you know." He ruffled his white hair with his hand, scooping off a layer of water. "And he told me that she's all right. And we'll see her again. Maybe even soon."

"Do you think we look the same, when we go over to the other side?" Rachel enquired.

"I don't know, chicky. But the Rescuer assures me I'll recognise your mother and we'll have all the time in the world to catch up. I reckon she's really proud of you. The lovely young lady you've become," said Eddie.

Rachel looked away. Her heart glowed.

Chapter 10

The sound of singing filled the basement of Lytescote Manor and crept up the stairs to the ground floor. Former generations used to fill the house with mirth and music. In Victorian times they would gather around the piano in the drawing room. This was, of course, before phones, tablets and flat screens. Sometimes, the children would entertain the adults with musical skits, compositions and classical favourites. Women would smile with their hands in their laps and men would sip strong drinks and smoke cigars. At other times, the old and young would croon together.

Even lately, Arabella had been fond of losing herself in music, enchanted by the grand piano. Sometimes Daniel would hear her beautiful tones fluttering through the house: like birds exploring the high-ceilinged mansion.

But the singing that filled the basement today was entirely different from that. This was a discordant, ugly shrieking. It came from Kumiko who was enjoying herself rather too much. The problem was, no one else enjoyed her singing: only her.

The soldier winced as the whip struck his back again. It made a cracking sound that entertained the muscle-bound Dream Fighter who was tasked with his beating. But the young soldier was submitted to his master's authority and knew he must take his punishment. Even if he didn't really deserve it.

On balance, he probably shouldn't have mentioned the passageway to Kumiko. If he'd kept it to himself, he would have avoided this beating. But then again, if the men were hiding down there, he would have been a hero. He'd taken his chances so he had to take the consequences of disappointing her.

Kumiko's singing turned into abusive screaming as her face contorted: "I hate you, you useless idiot. I hate this place. When is he coming? Why isn't he here yet?"

She pushed the torturer aside and drew blood from her prisoner with her fingernails.

"So, Samyaza can go to hell can he? Daniel Harcourt can go to hell! He can go there along with you!"

She quickly grew calm and stared at the young Dream Fighter. His hands were tied above his head with a rope, attached to a pulley. He was bleeding from his face, left side and back. Kumiko stroked his cheek gently.

"Shush," she commanded. "It's okay." Then she started to sing again. The notes were flat, truncated and high. The Dream Fighter screwed his face up as though about to cry. Given the choice of a beating or Kumiko's singing, he knew which one he'd rather have.

°°°°°12345°°°°°

For the Harcourt kids, the trip through this part of the mezzanine was like one long extended field trip, one huge adventure.

They chatted about all the places they'd visited in the mezzanine on this trip and the previous one.

"The chequer board, where your foot got stuck in the ground," said Rory.

"Ouch, yes. The caves which were dark and scary, and sound echoes round and round," replied Cameron. "The valley with the gaps that go down into the earth," he added.

"This forest with its big black trees, where it rains like a power shower!" said Rory.

Arabella chimed in, "I used to love an aqua spa in Seaclimb.

It has a set of showers that pretend to be different types of rain."

The boys listened hard, eyes like dinner plates.

"There's a Caribbean storm, together with sounds and smells of the beach. Another one is a storm at sea, mixing hot and cold water in, with fine and then painful jets of water spraying you unexpectedly!"

"I think the spa needs to make a mezzanine rain shower, with big hot bubbles of water, red and purple lighting, and the smell of a forest," Cameron suggested.

They emerged from the trees and found themselves in a huge open space. They were on the far right side of the fields where Rachel had been followed by the cheetah. Long tufty grass moved in the wind, ruffled under its caress. Every so often, it looked oceanic as it moved, undulating as the breeze grew fiercer. It resembled a rock star's mane of hair, tossed back and forth in time to the beat – except in slow motion.

The sky above held no rain clouds now and, instead, warm red sunlight poured down on them like a honey glaze over a cake. They soon dried out as they walked and enjoyed the heat of the strange, red sun.

"What do you call a sheep with no legs?" Lake asked Rory.

"I don't know."

"A cloud, of course!" Lake grinned. Rachel was glad that he'd returned to himself even if it meant putting up with his terrible jokes.

Everybody felt freer, no longer needing to look around every corner to see what kind of danger lurked there. The children ran through the long grass. Soon they outpaced the adults. They stopped some distance ahead, discovering a series of interesting nests where the grass was shorter. These were nestled into a patch of rounded lily pads that sat on thick, long stalks. They had translucent veins that emanated from their hearts and spanned outwards to their curved edges.

The boys started to poke them with a couple of sticks they found back in the forest.

"Boys, be careful," shouted Daniel from further up the field. He had a sense that not everything is as it seems in the mezzanine.

Rory cooed as a snake-like creature protruded upwards: a single, lengthy tentacle. It had two black round eyes, though no mouth that they could see. Suddenly, each nest had its own snake rising slowly out of it. They were milky white and slightly bristly. The boys were mesmerised.

Arabella caught up with them, rebuked them and told them to stand back.

"Listen, dear children. It really isn't clear whether these creatures are friends or foes. Do you understand me? So we really need to be careful and refrain from poking everything with a stick, unless we know for sure whether it wants to play or perhaps bite us? All right Cameron? Rory?"

They nodded, chastened, and walked away from the snakes which swayed in the air, thin tubular columns. However, Cameron and Rory did proceed more cautiously, for the time being, anyway.

°°°°°*12345*°°°°°

Rachel was walking hand-in-hand with Lake, swinging his arm up and down as they went and thoroughly enjoying herself. From time to time, she bashed his hand against his side, trying to annoy him. At one point, he grabbed her, held her tightly and kissed her on the lips.

"What was that for?" she giggled.

"Oh, I don't know. To make you stop," he smiled.

The ground beneath them was firm, and they crossed a field the size of several football pitches. It sloped down gently towards a stream. They swung their legs through the long grass, kicking it out of the way. It fell obediently: a stack of dominoes tumbling to the ground in their wake.

Rachel and Lake fell to the back of the crowd, leaving plenty of space between them and everyone else. She watched Caleb and Serena in the lead with their arms around each other. They looked so happy.

Trailing them were Daniel and Micah, deep in conversation. They didn't look troubled but were obviously trying to get to the bottom of some important matter or other. Scraps of conversation drifted back. They talked about history and politics and business. These were things that went over Rachel's head. Not that she was that interested anyway.

Arabella followed them with the kids. She wanted to make sure they didn't poke anything else and stayed safe. The children chattered and laughed.

Finally, Eddie marched, grinning and staring all around him like a toddler. He still hadn't got used to this place and seemed to marvel at every new wonder he discovered. He turned around every so often, regarding the horizon, watching the trees behind, and squinting at the river ahead which lined the rocky ridge that led to the caves. He wanted to take everything in and pack it deeply into his memory and imagination.

Lake relaxed even more, which was great. The personality that Rachel so adored shone through. He was being funny and charming, like when she met him. Just as he had been through the first year of their relationship.

It really wasn't his fault he had gone after Kumiko. Rachel had been the one who had pushed him away, with all her emotional issues: self-hatred, regrets, rage. She'd kept him at a distance. Anyone with half a brain would have run away from her – far away. But the old Rachel was gone now. That one was dead and buried. In her place was a new creation: someone who knew, deep down, that she was worth knowing and that Lake was lucky to be by her side.

Lake chatted away, telling her terrible jokes. He reminisced about Griffton, the sea, rollerblading, Griffton Cliff, things he enjoyed, things they'd done together. It was lovely.

"So," he said to her, "if the apocalypse doesn't happen, where would you like to live? Here or back in Griffton? Or maybe somewhere else? The world is our oyster, baby."

"Don't baby me. That's a great question. But I suspect things are going to come to an end. Either here in the mezzanine or back on Earth or both. All the signs and everything point to it. I don't understand the half of it. But from what Caleb says, the things that happened with Samyaza and the Malkin and all that, it's not looking good." She shuddered at the thought of Samyaza and his evil plan for humanity.

"You still haven't answered my question," Lake observed. "Just imagine that all this doesn't get rolled up and finished. Where do you fancy living? I quite like the look of that stream down there, near the caves. Looks pretty and quiet. Nice fresh water for fishing."

"Yes," said Rachel, "I've been there before. But I should warn you, Lake, that it may not be all it seems. It is a beautiful place but that's where one of those black creatures tried to attack me."

"So what happened?"

"Well, believe it or not, it flew down from on top of the caves over there. Then a big white angel appeared and stabbed it through the chest with a long sword. It happened this close to my face." She indicated the closeness with the palm of her hand.

"You're right. I don't really believe it. Though on second thoughts, I wouldn't put anything past this place. I'm not calling you a liar. I'm really not." He shook his head.

"Good for you, boy. Also, those caves over there. That's where Caleb's friends were killed. Eli and Anton. It was the shape shifter I told you about. Zed. He made himself look like Micah."

"That's horrible." Lake shivered and stared ahead of him. "Okay. Maybe we won't live here," he muttered.

A little later, Lake said to Rachel, "You seem different from how you used to be, Rachel."

"Yes," she agreed. "I feel stronger now. I'm a different person. It's amazing what happens when you settle with your past and find peace in the Rescuer."

"You keep talking about him as though he's a real person," said Lake.

Rachel smiled like a sphinx.

Chapter 11

They descended to the river with their travel packs and coats. Rachel was getting sick of carrying her jacket over her arm. It was becoming a burden. She would have thrown it away if she didn't think it would come in handy later when they got to Bhutan.

The river was wide here and its surface shimmered. It reflected the colours in the exotic sky which resembled a chessboard of clouds. Squares of pink cirrus cloud lay on a mauve backdrop. Down beneath it, by the river, purple and brown plants edged the water. Thick, tall grass grew out of the shallows in substantial fronds that spilled over onto the bank.

In the distance they could see the line of caves. Over there, knobbly grey-white rock lined the grassy edge of the stream. This section of caves lacked any entrances. The cave mouth was further down, a long hike away. That was the point where they had exited last time around and escaped from the horror that was the shape shifter and his spawners. The boys shivered when they thought about them and what had happened to Caleb's friends.

The group walked down the hill to the riverbank where there was a large build-up of green-grey mud. The boys quickly scrambled up it and stood, arms akimbo, staring back triumphantly at the travellers. The world was their climbing frame.

Caleb gathered everyone together. He jumped up on top of the muddy ridge, finding it firm underfoot.

"No, it's okay, boys. You don't have to get down. Why don't

you stay with me while I talk to everyone? We'll do it together," said Caleb. Naturally, the boys were thrilled.

The three of them stood on top of the bank in a line. They looked down at the others with Cameron on one side of Caleb and Rory on the other. They felt very important. Rory puffed out his chest and grinned.

"So, this is it, everyone. This is where we divide into three groups, right here and say our goodbyes."

"Really? Do we really have to split up so soon? It doesn't feel like we've had any warning! I've only just got to get to know you guys," Lake complained. He huffed and puffed a little bit. Rachel took his hand and calmed him down, whispering that he shouldn't make it hard for the boys. After all, they had grown fond of him too. Lake nodded and made his features neutral. They all settled down to listen to what Caleb had to say.

"Friends, we have important work to do, as you all know. This is where we must leave each other." He eyed Lake, who nodded and tried not to look unhappy.

"The task ahead of us is great, mostly because we do not know exactly what it entails or what lies ahead! But follow the Dunamis and he will guide you to your destination. He holds your destiny, and will light up your path."

"What we know is that there is a stone head for each of us to go through, a portal back to our world. You must listen carefully and seek guidance and counsel from the Dunamis because he will get you there, get you through and protect you. He will take you to the place where the Protectors live. When you get there, you will know what you need to do."

"Remember: be strong and very courageous. We will not be intimidated. Even when the enemy attacks most fiercely, which he will. Expect opposition. We are in a war. Stand firm in the Rescuer and in his mighty power. Do what the Dunamis tells you, and trust him always."

"Do you remember your groups? Of course you do. Serena, Micah, we are going through the caves. Much as I do not want to. That is the place where my friends are buried. That is the place where I was held prisoner, trapped in my nightmares, without hope. And my hope is that you are all spared that horror. But we must go through that way because the Dunamis is leading us there. So go we must. And we will not fear the darkness."

"Lake, Eddie and Rachel, you need to go right here, along the riverbank. It looks like it will get wider, so stay away from the edge unless you plan to have a bath! Serena and I both believe you are to follow it and keep going until you find your portal. We do not know how far you need to travel. We just know you need to follow the river and listen to the Dunamis' leading."

"Finally, the wonderful Harcourt family, so full of life, so full of love. Rory and Cameron, you are mighty warriors." He put his arms on their shoulders. "You are all so dear to me. You are to go in the opposite direction. That's where the river narrows to become a ravine and a brook in the distance. Follow it until it dries up and keep going along the wall of caves. We feel that you will know what to do, Daniel. Listen for the Rescuer's voice through his Dunamis and you will know."

Daniel nodded seriously.

"The work we will do on the other side, back on the Earth, is history changing. It will save lives and souls. I have no doubt about that. So, be courageous and be strong of heart and you will succeed. And if you happen to meet an angel, ask him whatever you want. Check you're on the right path. Ask whatever you can. They are our servants. And they are incredible to behold. I hope we will all meet them. Eddie and Lake, you haven't seen them yet, but you may do. When you do, your heart will be glad."

"When you get to your Protector, you will work out what to do. I have no more information for you. So stay close to the Dunamis and listen for his voice. Trust that he will tell you what you need to know, when you need to know it. This is how I have always lived my life since the first time I met him. And he has never let me down. Even when times have been tough. Very tough. Particularly of late. But I now understand why he put me through that test. My resolve is strong now."

Serena pulled him down off the hill gently and firmly. "Okay, I suppose you've heard enough from me!" he conceded. She whispered in his ear, and he said, "Ah, yes. She's right. Before we go our separate ways, why don't we spend some time with the Dunamis? Serena, you lead us."

Serena smiled at her husband and her eyes sparkled. She said in a musical voice, "I want everyone to listen out for the voice of the King. See if he prompts you to share anything, from the smallest of us, boys, to the biggest, Eddie. Please feel at liberty to share it. Cameron and Rory, why don't you just start singing to him, as you have so often on this journey? I love to hear you guys singing."

Boldly and from the bottom of their heart the boys sang a beautiful song to the Rescuer and his Dunamis. It was about his great love, and the glory of his presence.

The travellers sat down on the river bank. And as they did, Caleb said to them, "Why don't you just begin to welcome the presence of the Dunamis?"

Very soon, the Dunamis made his presence known. They encountered him as a river of peace that washed over them. Even Lake felt affected and tears came to his eyes. He rocked, remembering the feeling again from the house by the cliff last summer. It was a weight on his emotions, a supernatural force weighing him down and lifting him up simultaneously. He floated, borne aloft by the sweet presence of the King. His soul thirsted for it.

Nobody was in a hurry to move on, so they sat for some time with the Rescuer who renewed each of them. It almost felt as though he would appear any minute on his horse and climb down to sit with them. A great joy came over them, and they were filled with resolve for what lay ahead.

Serena said, "I feel that the Dunamis would remind us we are bullet-proof as long as he is with us. Without him we are nothing. With him, anything is possible. And when our time comes to leave this life behind, there is another life waiting for us, a life that will never end. One where there will be no sickness or death: we will be forever in the glory of his presence, dancing with angels."

Rory, who was sitting next to Lake, piped up, "Dear Rescuer, my friend. Thank you that evil men and bullies lose in the end. Thank you that you win. Help us to be strong when we meet the bad people. Even if they want to do us harm. And keep mum and dad and Cam safe."

Cameron added seriously, "Look after Micah as he goes off with Caleb and Serena. Keep him safe. We will miss him."

Lake whispered to Rory, "How do you do it? I'd like to have a go."

Rory turned to him and said quietly, "It's easy. You just talk to him. Talk to him like he's right here by the stream. Because he is."

Lake closed his eyes and said, "Rescuer. I'm Lake. But I guess you know that already. I just want you to know that I'm sorry about what happened back at the house. I didn't mean to be part of all the bad stuff. I hope you can forgive me if I ended up making things worse."

"I was wrong about Daniel. He's one of the good guys, and I got that wrong. I was wrong about Kumi as well. If you can do it, please change her mind about what she's doing. She's not as bad as she thinks she is. At least I don't think she is. Anyway, we all need your help. I need your help. Okay, this is Lake saying goodbye for now. And I hope I get to meet you because I really need you in my life. And I'd like to meet your horse too."

After a while, Caleb said in a loud voice, "In the name of the Rescuer and the Creator of all things, I cancel all assignments of the evil ones against us. I declare that your days are numbered, enemy, and you are powerless against the one who holds the world in the palm of his hand."

"I call on the angels to watch over us and protect us. Keep us on the narrow path that leads to the Protectors. Help us find them, and know how to activate them. We trust you, mighty

Rescuer, to lead us strongly with your Dunamis. Help us to do whatever you need us to do. Nothing more and nothing less. Help us all to be strong."

They lapsed into silence for a while, thinking, resting.

"Okay, everyone, it's time to go," Caleb pronounced.

He stood up, as did Daniel, and they hugged each other. "I am mightily proud of you," he said. "You have come a long way. Your past is well and truly behind you. Great things are ahead of you."

There were embraces all round. Rachel gave Arabella a long hug. They had grown fond of each other. Lake was sad to leave the boys, but everyone put on a brave face. Micah also found it hard to leave the Harcourt family but he also hid his emotions, shaking Daniel by the hand, and then being surprised as Daniel grabbed him by the shoulders and held him close.

Then they settled their backpacks on their backs. Eddie, Rachel and Lake departed in one direction. The bulk of the group went in the other. They would split again when they got to the cave mouth. At that point, Caleb, Serena and Micah would venture into the darkness, leaving the Harcourts to carry on under the violet sky.

The hunt for the three Protectors was underway.

Chapter 12

They walked along the riverbank with Eddie ahead of them, leading confidently. To the left of the river, a dark wall of angular rock rose up. Hand-sized slabs jutted out: cuboid projections that reflected the red sky. Furry moss lined the rocks' vertical edges.

The foaming waters raced in front of them. It felt to Rachel like the water was urging them on. They passed a couple of black rocks poking out of the river. They were moist at the top as the water splashed upwards in its haste.

Eddie ran ahead to inspect some turquoise and aquamarine flowers. They had five petals and a dark centre and resembled earthly geraniums. Their tall stems poked out of the soil at the edge of the river and Eddie stopped dangerously close to the ridge to look.

"Dad," called Rachel but he was off again.

"Is there anything else that you haven't told me?" Rachel asked Lake.

He looked guilty. Rachel let him stew for a few moments. She wondered how far things had really gone with Kumiko. Several emotions rose up that Rachel really didn't want inside her. Jealousy, regret, frustration. She breathed in and asked the Dunamis to help. A calmness descended upon her. She was learning how to grab hold of and tame her thoughts and hand them over to him. It meant she could maintain her peace. It was a constant struggle but it was getting easier by the day. She was learning so many new things with the help of the Dunamis. As each day passed, he was creating a better version of herself.

After a while, Lake said thoughtfully, "I did stop by at Iona's house."

"My friend Iona?"

"She's my friend too."

"No she isn't."

"Well, she is now."

"Whatever. So what made you 'stop by' at Iona's house then? By the way, she did mention it to me."

"Oh, you know." He stared at the rushing water.

"No I don't. That's why I'm asking." Rachel regretted being so snappish with him. So she softened her face and listened patiently.

"Things got bad in Griffton. You weren't around, and I don't mean that in any blaming way. But basically, everyone wanted to check on their friends. The guys at the paper, you know. The reality is I don't really have that many friends outside work, ha ha! Anyway, I remembered where she lived. Iona. I wanted to check she was okay because people were going so crazy. They were breaking into houses. Nicking things. And really hurting people. Even just for kicks."

"Yeah, I know. It sounded horrendous."

"So anyway, she was still on crutches after the accident. Ben closed Rock and Shock after it got smashed up. You probably knew about that?"

Rachel nodded.

"I showed her your note. Kumiko's note I mean. I was trying to make some sense of it all. She thought you went to Birmingham too."

"That Kumiko," spat Rachel. But that was all she said.

They walked on in silence.

"So, how is she – Iona I mean?" asked Lake.

"Oh, I caught up with her yesterday. I introduced her to the Rescuer. The Dunamis healed her leg. She's completely better now," said Rachel quietly.

"Really? You did that?" Lake's eyes were like table tennis balls.

"No, he did it. It wasn't me." She looked ahead at her father with his white hair. He was her father and she loved him. It just flowed out of her heart, whereas before she had only felt contempt or indifference for him.

Just then, Eddie turned back.

"Kids," he called. "It looks like the river runs out over there."

"What you mean?" Lake demanded. But he could see that the broad river was rushing underneath a wall of dark rock. An extension of the series of caves, the rock overhung the river. It was fat and tall and swallowed the water up greedily.

"How can that happen?" yelled Lake. "How are we going to follow it now?"

Eddie ran ahead, alarmed that the river refused to emerge again. The path continued but no longer wound alongside the waters. In the distance, even the rocks ran out and gave way to scrubland.

"How can we follow the river if there's nothing to follow?" he said in desperation. Further ahead, the path forked in three directions. One of them led straight on, but the others went away across open space. One was at right angles and the other at forty-five degrees. The right-angled one led towards the fields that eventually took them back to the forest where the rain had fallen. That was clearly the wrong way. The other two paths went on and on, their destination unclear.

"This is ridiculous," Lake complained.

"Dunamis," Rachel said. "Which way now?" She waited.

There were no words in her spirit.

"What does he say?" Lake enquired. "Did he say anything? Is the river going to come back?"

Rachel looked into his eyes. "I don't hear anything," she said impassively.

"We should carry on going in a straight line," Eddie commanded. "It's the most logical option."

"Do you think logic has anything to do with this place?" asked

Lake, waving his arms.

"I think Dad's right."

"So, this is a Race thing, is it?"

"Don't try to be funny."

"Coz he's Eddie Race and you're Rachel Race," he continued.

"Just shut up, Lake."

Eddie charged ahead, continuing along the path at pace. The decision was made. His feet kicked up a small cloud of grey dust.

"What are you waiting for?" Lake said to Rachel.

They travelled silently for a long time, passing through the scrubland and scuffing their shoes on tough weeds and mounds of stony soil. In this part of the mezzanine, the ground was copper coloured with chocolate streaks.

A couple of hundred metres ahead lay a forest. A cluster of gargantuan tree trunks, the colour of cinnamon bark, stood to attention. A canopy of branches fanned out many feet above the ground. With their arms interlocked they blocked out much of the light from the swirling, purple sky.

A persistent breeze blew, ruffling their clothes. It carried the smell of smoky charcoal on its wings. Pterodactyls circled above, darting into the pink beetroot clouds. The puffy, cumulus clouds hid them for a time before they shot out of the other side.

The creatures looked like tiny plastic toys, being so far up. Lake remembered a collectable set of dinosaurs he owned when he was five. What happened to that set? He was sure it wasn't being stored in the attic. How can things just disappear? Maybe his parents had given them to charity. He hoped they went to a good home, just like in Toy Story.

Then his thoughts turned to Daniel, Caleb and the rest. "I wonder how the others are doing," he said to himself.

Hearing him, Rachel replied, "Let's hope they found their stone head."

"Me too. And let's hope we find ours as well."

"What do you think that is over there?" Lake pointed to something black in the distance, over to their left. It looked like the outline of a large bat.

"Hang on. Is that what I think it is?"

Rachel froze. "I've seen that before." Then she screamed: "Dad, run for the trees. It's a demon!"

Lake's face fell. He stood, rooted to the spot. He stared at the creature. It appeared to look back at him. He gasped as it spread its wings. Its wingspan was enormous. It lifted slowly off the ground like a Harrier Jump Jet. Then it settled back down again.

But they weren't taking any chances. "Run Lake! They move fast. We need to make it to those trees."

Lake shook himself off. He joined them in sprinting to the forest. They leapt with ease over stones and bushes. Lake bounced on the balls of his feet.

Eddie made it to the tree line. Lake outpaced Rachel. Her face was frozen, her eyes locked on the goal. He grabbed her hand and they ran together the rest of the way. No one dared to look back.

They hid themselves between the tree trunks, frozen like figurines. Panting, Lake stared out at the path and then the sky. He couldn't see it anymore. He checked every rock and every shrub, scanning left to right like a Terminator.

"Where is it?" He said, panic in his voice.

"I can't see it. I don't know where it's gone," said Eddie, eyes darting back and forth. He pushed Rachel behind him, hiding her deeper in the forest. After so many years of wanting to protect her and failing, he would do things right this time. If he had to take a bullet for her, it was a done deal. And if a demon should decide to strike, he would stand so she could run. He couldn't prevent the Malkin from swiping at her face. But next time, he would be ready.

His eyes fell upon a group of rocks. Could it be there? He balled his hands into fists. His jaw was rigid. Yes, it was definitely something.

"Look, I can see something moving. Over there."

They all fixed their eyes on the set of rocks. There it was. A black head in the distance, bobbing up and down. They huddled together as two wings appeared on either side of the rocks. Then, with a shriek, it launched itself into the air. Without stopping, it soared towards the clouds.

Rachel laughed out loud. "It's one of those bird things," she said loudly.

"A pterodactyl," added Lake.

"Yes. And it's gone." She watched it as it disappeared. Then it re-emerged in the sky and circled with a couple of its friends.

Lake sat on the ground. "Well, that's a relief," he said. But he found it hard to smile.

Eddie kept watch as they rested, never taking his eyes off the horizon or the group of rocks in the distance.

"Yeah, it's a relief," he agreed. "But they are out there."

°°°°°*12345*°°°°°

On the move again, they passed through the forest and out through the other side. It was starting to grow dark now. The strange red sun-moon was slipping slowly down to the ground. It was on a slow and unrelenting journey. At the end of its track it would steal the light from today. The mezzanine world would be turned to darkness. Meanwhile, as it retreated, the sun set fire to the feathery stratus clouds. They were already burning pink and purple. But the sun added yellow and orange flames to their soft edges.

Eddie smiled in wonder. He loved watching sunsets back home, but these were so much better. The creative mind behind such beauty was far too large for him to fathom, he thought. The Creator's mind.

He fell into conversation with Rachel and Lake.

"Beautiful, isn't it?" he remarked.

"Sure is," said Lake.

"I remember a time when I thought all this was random – purposeless. The world, I mean."

"Go on, Dad," said Rachel.

"It's like the Dunamis is giving me a deep understanding of the things of the universe," Eddie continued.

"So, the way I see it, the Creator set in motion a system: a highly complex system. It's got immense beauty and mystery in it, and freedom for its creatures - us."

"Okay," nodded Lake.

"We experience great autonomy: the ability to choose what to do with each of our moments. Moments are vitally important. In my case, whether to pick up the bottle or put it down."

"Put it down. Definitely put it down," said Rachel, with a twinkle in her eye.

"Whether to react, or pause and respond. The Dunamis explained to me that character is forged in the moment. Battles are won and lost. Every choice moves us towards or away from the Rescuer. In my case, many of my choices pushed me further away from the King. I didn't even know about him in the past, though I suspect your mother did. And then I met him and he changed everything."

"So, if it's such a beautiful world, why so much pain? Why do people die young and suffer so badly? Why doesn't the Creator step in and fix things?"

"The Creator could intervene directly. He has the power. But having set in motion an autonomous world, he chooses to work with his creatures' natures and inclinations. And he knows what's in the heart of a man. He knows what my heart is like," said Eddie. "Meanwhile, we all grow up together like flowers or weeds. I used to be a weed. But since I met the Rescuer, my life turned from weeds to flowers."

"I know what you mean," smiled Rachel.

Eddie continued, "It was because of him – the Rescuer. He is flowers. He's the fragrance, the beauty, the purity of flowers. And something happened – an exchange – which meant my weeds were swapped for flowers. The weeds I'd spent my life growing. But those weeds are dead and gone and the King turned my brown hair white so I'd never forget."

Rachel leant over and ruffled his hair.

"And with my white hair, I gained a relationship with the Creator of the universe who loves me for who I am." Eddie stared into the distance.

He carried on talking but he was talking to himself now, not his two companions. "I can still remember what it was like to know the world as random, starkly scientific - where people evolved from nothing by accident. A world where order comes from chaos. Intelligent life springs up from the dust. It lives, loves, thinks, feels. But now I think that point of view needs an equal amount of faith."

"The words of the Rescuer often come to my mind. I fell into the lake, down that canyon. And I was saved by you, Rachel, because you're such a good swimmer. The Rescuer took me away on his white horse. He told me, 'I have chosen you and adopted you into my family, like a son. Everything I have is now yours. But it's not because of anything good you've done. You're not going to get everything right, Eddie. Nor do you have to. No, it's because I love you. So relax and follow me.' And so I did, and so I am."

°°°°°*12345*°°°°°

Beyond the forest, they crossed a plain surrounded by low black mountains. Similar to the previous one, it was specked with rocks and hardy weeds. There were no enemies in sight. The sun sent long streaks upwards into the sky. The group was very aware that darkness would soon engulf them. They would need to look for a place to camp and keep watch.

Miraculously, the river appeared again. It flowed out from underground and picked up as though it had never gone away. They stood and marvelled at the river mouth. In effect, the plain and the forest had acted as an expansive bridge. They had probably been walking on top of the water without realising it.

"We've been following the river all along and we didn't even know it!" said Eddie delightedly.

Lake smiled to himself. "It was the right decision after all. I never doubted it."

Rachel looked at him and smirked. "Okay, where next?"

"Follow the river!" cried Eddie. "We carry on following the river. That's what the Dunamis told Serena. And that's good enough for me."

"All right Dad. Lead on then."

Eventually, the water wound around to the right. But the path became increasingly difficult to tread. Sharp rocks poked upwards, hurting their feet. Not only were their edges serrated but their surfaces were knobbly: painful to walk on. In addition, the ground became gappy. Fist-sized holes opened up. They threatened to trap their feet. A twisted ankle here would mean enforced rest and they knew time was of the essence. They needed to reach their stone head and activate the Air Protector as soon as possible. Nobody knew exactly how or why. But they knew it would be profoundly helpful back on Earth.

Just when the route became impossible to continue, they came to a bridge over the river. It was a natural bridge, not man made. It was too uneven to be hewn by human hands. Their choice was clear. They could scramble slowly over the jagged rocks. It would take time and tear the skin on their hands and legs. Or they could cross the bridge that led over the fast-flowing river. It was beset by cracks but it was the only logical option available. They would still be following the river, but on the other side.

They looked at each other under the glow of the purple sky.

"The bridge it is," Eddie decided.

As they approached it they were arrested by an unnerving sight. It was the pale skull of a beast, wedged onto a branch through its eye socket. The stumpy tree grew out of the bank near the bridge.

Lake looked at the rounded eye holes of the skull and the way the cranium was etched with thin brown lines. Parts of the rounded head were brown and yellow. The animal's yellow teeth protruded from its long jawbone which was curved into a snarl.

"A deer?" he guessed.

"That looks like a fox," said Eddie.

"Whatever it is, someone or something killed it and hung it on that branch," said Lake. He shivered, looking across the bridge nervously.

Chapter 13

"I'm not going over there," said Lake, shakily. He lay down his pack and coat. His piercing, hazel eyes were wide open. He ruffled his treacle-coloured hair distractedly with his hand. It was in need of a cut, thought Rachel. Or certainly a tidy up.

"What you mean?" Rachel demanded. "We can't carry on going over those rocks. It's impossible. Just look at them."

"It just looks too dangerous. Crossing the river. Besides, aren't we meant to follow it?"

"We will follow it. Just from the other side."

"We're not asking you to jump in the river," Eddie laughed. "It's just a bridge."

"I can't do it."

"Why on earth not, man?"

"I can't explain it. I just don't want to do it." In his mind, Lake had locked onto a distant memory from his childhood. He was sailing with his father. A squall blew up unexpectedly around their tiny boat. The intense gusts brought a wave over their heads. He was carried into the deep waters. Despite his buoyancy aid, he went under. It was the most terrifying moment of his life. He couldn't remember being rescued by his father. All he could recall now was the terror he'd felt.

"This is not the Lake I know. You went undercover with the Zodiacs, remember? You do stupid things like work for that dangerous criminal Kumiko," Rachel scoffed.

Lake stared at her as though she were mad.

"You do crazy rollerblading tricks. You throw yourself down steep hills and slide down handrails. This is just a bridge over a river. Look, I'll hold your hand as we cross, you little baby."

"Yeah, you two lovebirds can hold hands," Eddie laughed. "I can see a great place to spend the night on the other side. It's sheltered and we can wait by those rocks until morning comes. It looks safe enough."

Eddie placed his foot on the bridge. It was made of interconnected slabs of rock. They looked like they had grown together organically, though there were gaps and cracks between them. The path was narrow. There were no handrails. To Eddie it looked straightforward enough.

But as soon as he'd gone a few steps he turned back and said, "He's right. I'm not sure I can do it either."

He backed away from the bridge and rejoined them on the bank. He had to choose his steps carefully because it was now dark.

"What do you mean, Dad?" Rachel asked in exasperation.

"I'm scared," he said, flatly. "I'm scared, girl. I don't know why."

"Would you listen to yourself? You can see the other side. It's just over there! It's not far to go. You're not going to fall off. Besides, the water doesn't look that deep. Come on, take a deep breath and follow me boys." She imagined herself taking this tone and approach with Rory and Cameron. Not her father and a nineteen-year-old man.

Rachel set off, holding Lake's hand. Reluctantly, Lake and Eddie followed her. Their steps were short and tentative. It was like they were drugged.

"You can do it," she encouraged them. But her heart started to falter. She could feel panic coming over her. It was like a watercolour brush was stroking wet paint over her body from her face down to her knees. Thoughts attacked her mind. There were monsters everywhere. Unseen dangers were poised, ready to pounce. Ferocious beasts were about to leap up onto the bridge and drag them down into the river. Demons hid in the rocks beyond the bridge. They were waiting to leap onto her back and sink their teeth into her neck. The thoughts were paralysing.

Halfway across the bridge, she saw a creature through the gap. It was hanging onto the underside of the bridge. Through the spaces between the rocks she observed its smooth, bulbous mass. It was lit by the glow from above. It was one of the huge spider creatures from the caves. Those horrible translucent monsters that sat on top of the heads of Caleb and his friends. These dark creatures feed you a diet of nightmares and take away your hope. They steal your joy and give you despair in its place. They were big round sacks of evil, wicked nightmare monsters. And they were centimetres away from her feet.

She let out a high-pitched scream and recoiled in horror. The surface of its skin was smooth and rubbery. A cold dread descended on her. Her fear was evolving from a quiet panic to a fully-fledged horror. She jumped as she spotted another creature further along the bridge. Then a third one. There was a row of them, lying in wait.

She couldn't do it. There was no way they could cross the bridge. The danger was too great. She saw what these things did to Caleb, Anton and Eli. And they were grown men, seasoned followers of the Rescuer and his Dunamis. They had to go back.

"Rescuer, help!" she gulped.

Her fear lifted for a moment. Gripped by a boost of faith and a superhuman resolve, she lifted her shoe up and stamped down hard on the bridge. Her foot landed right over the place where the first spider octopus was holding on. The feel of hard stone jarred her knee.

"Careful!" shouted Lake.

Rachel stamped again. In her mind, she was killing a big spider in the bathroom. It was girl against monster, and girl was born to win. The creature quickly released its grip on the stones in response to the barrage. It tumbled straight down – a plump apple dropping from a tree – and splashed into the impatient waters that were waiting to receive it.

Encouraged by her triumph, Rachel ran and jumped over the next one. She landed hard with both feet and it had the desired effect. It too relinquished its grasp. The third one fell likewise. The river took them far downstream, bobbing and rolling as they went. The three travellers watched them speedily float away, ecstatic at Rachel's success.

Immediately, the sense of fear lifted. Rachel laughed. The others relaxed. Eddie put his arm around Lake. They stood confidently, having joined Rachel on the bridge.

"I am literally speechless," said Lake.

"Yes, she really is something isn't she?" commented Eddie. Rachel grinned. Lake looked at her, seeing her white teeth shining under the glow of the mezzanine sky.

"Yes, she sure is."

"Let's not get complacent though," Eddie pointed out. "We should cross over to solid ground."

"Sure, Dad!" Something Daniel once told her came to her mind. He said it was something Caleb had taught him. "Our struggle is not against flesh and blood. It's against the rulers, the authorities, and the powers of this dark world, and against the spiritual forces of evil in the spiritual realms."

So often, she reflected, the battle was in the mind and in the heart – the emotions. But if she had learned one thing, it was that the Rescuer had given her the power to overcome.

°°°°°12345°°°°°

Back in Griffton, Kumiko was on the rampage. Her long black hair was matted and awry. Her eyes blazed with passion. Unusually, she hadn't taken her morning shower and was dressed in her gym clothes: grey sweat pants with an orange T-shirt. Also unusually for her, she was without make-up. Her face was bare and plain, pale and sickly.

The Dream Fighters were the last people who would tell her

about her body or breath odours. The way she smelt stale and acrid. She was in good company. These were men for whom personal hygiene was low on the list.

"Burn it down! Burn it down!" she shrieked. "Burn the city down building by building."

"Where would you like us to start, Master?" asked the Dream Fighter Commander.

"Oh, I don't care. How about the Griffton News? The place where he works. Emerson. Why don't you burn that one down?"

"I'm pleased to say, Miss Starkweather, that we have already completed that request."

"Of course, of course. Did it burn well? I know everything is digital these days. But newspapers still have plenty to burn. The clue is in the name – news 'papers'," she smiled wickedly. "Proofs and papers, printouts and pictures. Loads to burn."

"Yes Master. The Griffton News went down quickly. Unfortunately, being night-time, casualties were minimal. A couple of other buildings caught fire though, which is good."

"That's fine. Not a problem. At least the rat won't have anywhere to run. What's next? Why not Griffton Library? That's got loads of stuff that will catch fire. Books and magazines and wooden shelves. I've always hated books anyway. I wasn't alive when they burned all the books. I wish I was. I'll come and watch this time. It will be fun. We should bring marshmallows on sticks. We can toast them in the fire."

The Commander looked at her without showing any signs of emotion. He was a barrel-chested man with a thick moustache and eyes that were hard to read. He recognised that his job was to do her bidding and only speak or give an opinion if asked.

This was such a time. "What do you think?"

"Me, Miss Starkweather?"

"Yes you, you idiot."

"I think the library is an excellent idea." He ignored her insult and allowed himself a thin smile. "Lots, as you say, to burn."

"Good. We'll blame the Rescuer-followers again. I never get

tired of that. Get it organised. Call me when you're about to start. I'll come down on my bike. You bring the marshmallows."

The Commander waited patiently.

"What are you waiting for? These are orders," shouted Kumiko.

"Right away Master."

"Wait a moment."

"Miss Starkweather?"

"Do you have any hobbies?"

"Say again?"

"Hobbies. Things you like to do. Do you have any? I used to collect insects when I lived in Asia. And I like my bikes. How about you? What do you like doing?"

"I'm not really sure I could say."

"Okay. Get out then."

As he turned to leave, he heard Kumiko saying, "When are you coming, my dear Sammy? Why aren't you here yet? Damn you. I need you. I long for you. I can't do this on my own. It's the people. They make me crazy. I just want to kill them all."

°°°°°°*12345*°°°°°°

Eddie, Rachel and Lake spent the night on the other side of the bridge. They wedged their backs against the rocks and sat on a mossy carpet. The winter coats acted as cushions behind them. Their rucksacks were piled up by their feet.

They took turns keeping watch. Rachel was first, with Lake taking second watch and Eddie rounding off the night and leading them into early morning. They all took their responsibilities very seriously, particularly Lake.

Mercifully the night passed without event. On her watch, however, Rachel thought she saw eyes staring at her from across the water. They looked at her without blinking for close to an hour. This unnerved her at first. She relaxed after it became clear she wasn't going to be attacked.

It gave her the opportunity to talk to the Dunamis. As she

spent time with him, she felt calm and protected. From time to time, the eyes faded and became part of the darkness. Then, they returned. But they never approached.

In fact, during the whole night nothing confronted them. They were accompanied by the soothing sound of the river flowing by. When her turn came to rest, she fell into a black slumber. It was reminiscent of the time she had been drugged by Zed in his wooden tumbledown house.

As she started to snooze, she tried to think of the strangest place she'd ever fallen asleep. It might have been in the wardrobe at Grandpa's big house in Solihull. Or it might have been that time when she followed the lights to Griffton Cliff and woke up with her feet in the sea.

She felt that, on that occasion, the enemy had tried to kill her but the angels had saved her instead. Her theory was that instead of falling off the cliff, they had carried her over the rooftops and placed her gently on the beach.

Soon, her thoughts became cloudy. The dark undercurrents of sleep dragged her under and kept her there for a long time. Fortunately, she woke up clearheaded and rejuvenated.

"Is anyone hungry?" Eddie asked in a hoarse voice. Lake sat staring blearily. He shook his head. Rachel smiled and straightened his hair with her fingers.

"I'm not either," she said.

"Okay then. Why don't we move on? Here comes the sun."

In no time they were walking along the river again. The unwelcoming terrain continued on the other side. If anything, it got worse. Shards of rock stuck out of the high bank. Walking over that would cause serious injuries.

The foaming river sang a whispering tune to them, elucidated by the Dunamis. For Rachel it was a tune about lost tribes and ancient battles. It hinted at eternal creatures that predated humans: the angelic host and the fallen ones. There were realities and certainties beyond the grasp of her mind. She caught a glimpse of a world far greater than one she could ever have imagined. It was one of which she could only observe a fraction.

The landscape suddenly changed. The rocks on both sides of the water grew mossy and smooth. There were more plants. Some of them were made of clusters of round red leaves. Others were long and spiky, jade in colour. Yet others had fur around their edges the colour of amethysts.

The water was relatively clear, reddy-purple under the bizarre sky. Lake wondered whether the water was safe to drink. He heard a chirping sound which he assumed was coming from some sort of hidden creatures. For the next hour or two they all tried to spot a new form of alien life. But the creatures were camouflaged or very good at hiding.

This part of the journey seemed to last for hours. Then they hit an unexpected problem.

"Oh, I don't believe it," Lake exclaimed. They had spied it in the distance and wondered about it as they approached. It now halted them in their tracks. Just like before, the river carried on going, but it rushed under an insurmountable stone cliff. There was no way to get past it.

On the other bank, which was too far away, and too high to climb, lay a blanket of spiky rocks that would surely pierce their shoes. Over to the left was a thick, high column of stone that stretched for miles behind them and joined the rocks that ate up the water.

"We're stuck," Eddie admitted. "Maybe we took a wrong turning further back. Maybe 'follow the river' meant follow it to start with and then move away from it. I don't know."

Lake sat down on the path and crossed his arms.

"There has to be a way," said Rachel, optimistically.

"Really? Why don't you ask your Dunamis? He could blow a hole through the rock for us," said Lake sarcastically. "Or maybe he'll teleport us to the stone head."

"I don't know. But I reckon there's a way. We just need to ask him and wait."

Chapter 14

Rory and Cameron were completely immersed in the game they were playing. Basically, you got one point if you spotted a round frog creature. They had come across so many that they were only worth one. You got two points if you could find a blue flower because most of them had been purple or red so far. And you got five thousand points if you saw a pterodactyl in the sky.

Rory was winning but only because he'd spotted two pterodactyls. He was adamant that it wasn't the same one flying overhead twice, and Cameron eventually agreed. This skewed the score in his favour.

Shouldering their packs like two seasoned adventurers, they strode ahead of their parents. It gave Daniel and Arabella time to talk without being interrupted. It also meant they could keep their eyes on the boys.

The series of uneven caves was extraordinarily long. It ran for miles and towered above them. Every so often the family came upon a smooth cave mouth. They always approached them with some trepidation. They didn't know what might be hiding inside. Daniel would go first, stepping forward and looking inside to check there wasn't any immediate danger lurking there.

And to think, mused Daniel, he might have been that danger in the past. Samyaza used to get him to conceal himself somewhere and cause somebody a scare. But that life was over.

From time to time, they saw huge gaping holes higher up in

the shadowy rock. On occasion they stared down like the eyes of a vast skull. Daniel speculated about how they might have been formed. They could have been caused by erosion, or equally blasted out by missiles. There was no way of truly making sense of the geology of the mezzanine.

The river disappeared a long way back, as Caleb had predicted. It changed from being a river to a ravine and then a brook. They had all enjoyed walking alongside the water. Its sound was delightful as it tripped over pebbles and stones.

As it thinned, they saw more and more creatures: spherical floating frogs and amphibians that didn't live in bubbles. The boys spotted a couple of scarlet snakes. There were even long spiky insects hiding in the weeds. After the water dried up, there were no creatures to see. There were only stones and dust and the odd growth. They crunched the dry ground underfoot. Round stones became tiny footballs to kick about.

Daniel and Arabella were talking about school, home and work.

"I recognise that life will never be the same as it was before. But it seems such a shame. I did love that house, and the boys were really enjoying school," Arabella said, sadly. "I wonder how everyone is doing. Our friends I mean. And Marie-Michelle. It's a good thing that Cam and Rory get on so well. They don't seem to miss their school friends."

"I know, Bella. The great thing is that we are together. But, do you know what? I sense we're nearing the end of days now," Daniel commented. "Things are winding down, heating up, breaking apart. However you want to put it. Lytescote Manor is the least of our worries. Oh, did I tell you? I electrified the toilets and the water tank when I went back for Lake."

Arabella smiled. "That will teach them to trample on my Persian rugs," she quipped. Daniel leant over and kissed her on the cheek.

Do you think we will ever get it back? The house. Honestly, my grandfather would have been mortified. I suppose everybody has to make sacrifices."

"Yes. I don't know. Do we really want it back after they've finished with it?"

"What do you think Samyaza wants?" she asked, thoughtfully.

"What does he ever want? What Samyaza wants is to steal man's adoration and praise for himself. He wants total devotion. He wants the world to worship him, that's what he wants. And if he can't get his way through temptation, he'll try to get it through manipulation or force. And failing that, he will destroy everyone and everything. Which is why we must stop him."

°°°°°12345°°°°°

The group climbed for a couple of miles. Every so often, Daniel put his hand out against the rough rocks to steady himself. The line of rocks started to curve away, leading them in a broad semicircle. Obediently, the Harcourt family kept close, walking alongside their ever-present companion: the caves.

But then they petered out. They changed from being colossal and overhanging to being a high wall made of rough rock. Then they shrank down further to the point where the boys could climb on top and walk along a flat ridge. Then they just ended, leaving open space on all sides. It was late evening in the mezzanine. The same sun that had set fire to the low-lying clouds above Rachel, Eddie and Lake was doing the same over the heads of the Harcourts. The children marvelled at the colours, cooing and pointing.

"Which way, Dan?" Arabella enquired.

"I don't feel that we should go back the way we came. That's what would happen if we followed these rocks round." He put his hands on his hips and looked across the plain. "I think we should go that way. Follow the line that the rocks would have made if they carried on going."

"But I don't see anything."

"Neither do I. But it's worth a go."

"Are you sure, Daniel?"

"Yes. I'm sure," he said confidently.

As they progressed across the plain, it was unclear whether it was a good decision or a bad one. The ground became uneven and difficult to negotiate. As it grew darker, there were more and more gaps in the ground that led down into the inky blackness.

"Dan, this isn't good," said Arabella. "I don't think we've gone the right way. The kids are finding it too difficult. Besides, it's getting a little bit too dark to see, do you not think?"

"Okay, maybe we should stop for the night. We could set off when it's light again."

"But there isn't anywhere to stop. Nowhere safe, anyway."

"Let's go for a bit longer. Maybe we'll find a place to rest in a while."

"It's your decision, honey."

Keeping the children close to them, they ventured slowly across the darkening plain. Eventually, it became problematic to see the holes in the ground properly, though the red glow from the sky made the stones around them visible.

They made it to a large group of rocks and sat down. Fortunately, it was possible to lean their backs against these boulders, and the kids were happy enough. The tall rocks also gave them some shelter, concealing them from prying eyes across the plain. Within minutes of stopping, the boys were snoozing happily. Arabella put her arm around Rory. His head lolled onto Cameron's shoulder.

Daniel and Arabella spent the night watching out for predators. There was no movement out there but they remained vigilant.

°°°°°12345°°°°°

Daniel found that he had fallen into a quiet sleep. He shook himself off, to find the boys arguing with each other. This was unusual, though not unexpected. They were living under some degree of pressure to get to their destination. And they didn't

111

really know where their destination was or how long they had to reach it.

Rory was shouting at Cameron. "You're a stupid loser!"

"I hate you, you idiot," Cameron screamed back.

"Boys, calm down."

"You shut up," Rory spat at him. "I don't have to listen to you. You're an idiot as well."

"Yes you do. I'm your father. You will do as I tell you," he commanded forcefully. The sun was up, bathing the cracked rocks in a red blush. It lit up the holes in the path ahead: the ones that fell away into the ancient abyss that lay beneath the mezzanine.

"What's going on, Bella?"

"It's all your fault Daniel," Arabella said unkindly. "You're never around. You're always away from home, working on your security projects. No wonder they turned out the way they did."

"What are you talking about? They're great kids!" Daniel protested.

"They're chips off the old block: sneaky, secretive and horrible," she said. "In fact, I've had it with the lot of you. You can all go to hell!"

"Really, Bella. This is not you."

"Don't you 'Bella' me, Danny Boy."

Just then, Cameron screamed from deep inside his small body and tore off across the hazardous plain. He hopped from stone to stone, leaping across the gaps, his backpack bouncing as he leapt.

"Well? Aren't you going to go after him?" she demanded.

Daniel stood for a moment and stared at his family. He grabbed his pack and loped off after his oldest son, trying to reason with him as he went. "Cam, come back. We can work this out."

By the time he caught up with Cameron, the boy was calm. A puzzled look crossed his youthful face.

Daniel hugged him close and they turned to look back at Arabella and Rory. The two of them were having a heated exchange. Rory waved his arms and Arabella stood close and yelled into his face.

Cameron screamed and pointed past them. He gesticulated towards something that was sitting just beyond the rocks where they had rested.

"Over there. Look! Monsters!" yelled Rory.

Everyone stopped and turned to look at the rocks. Two round spider creatures squatted at their base, their bulbous, see-through heads glowing a dark purple colour under the morning sun. Their skin was smooth and featureless like the surface of a balloon.

Arabella screamed. She grabbed Rory by the arm and lifted up their two packs with the other hand. She immediately shot away from the rocks, bringing her possessions with her. The shock of seeing the creatures snapped her out of her rage. Only one desire filled her mind. She wanted to put as much distance between her and the things as possible.

As soon as the family was reunited, they embraced each other and wept. Arabella turned and glared at the rocks. The rotund beings stayed where they sat, in the distance where they belonged.

"This place is a nightmare. I am so sorry, Daniel," she cried. "You are a good father. I didn't mean anything I said back there."

"It's okay. No need to apologise. It wasn't you. It wasn't us. The enemy is prowling around. They want us to attack each other. It's how they win."

She looked into his eyes and they connected again.

"This place is full of surprises. We have to be on our guard," added Daniel.

The family walked sombrely, hand-in-hand, away from the sinister spiders. Daniel wondered what horror was in store for them next.

°°°°°12345°°°°°

They walked uphill for a long time. The ground was firmer here and less treacherous. They hadn't been particularly vigilant, just chatting quietly about nothing in particular. Then it appeared in the distance.

"That's it! That's our stone head! And I saw it first," Cameron called out.

First, they thought it was another rock. Then they started to make out its shape. The jaw line. The thick brow. Finally, the deep-set eyes came into view. It stood in the middle of nowhere: a field of red, Martian soil. Small black trees, the size of children, specked the landscape on either side. And there it was in their midst.

"I never thought I'd be so pleased to see one of those," breathed Arabella.

Daniel smiled a huge smile. "We made it through the mezzanine. Thank goodness we made it through in one piece. Now to find our Protector. Pacific island, here we come!"

Naturally, the kids ran ahead. They raced each other to see who would be the first to reach the goal. Cameron had slightly longer legs, so was able to outpace his brother initially. But he stumbled on a loose stone and lost the advantage. Encouraged, Rory sped ahead. Cameron tended to win their races, though Rory was determined. Consequently, he sometimes had the ability to win the longer races through sheer willpower.

"Wait for us, boys," urged Arabella.

There was still a long way to go until they reached the stone monolith. Daniel expected the boys to run out of steam and walk the rest of the way. At that point, they would be able to catch them up.

He felt a breeze on his face and looked up. The sound of wings filled the air. Three black leathery creatures soared overhead. But these were no pterodactyls. They were talon-wielding, thick-bodied demons, reminiscent of giant bats. They made a throaty noise that was a cross between a hiss and a roar. It filled Daniel with dread. He looked back at his boys, ashen-faced. Arabella was screaming incessantly, chasing hard after the boys.

Rory looked up, terror in his eyes. He put his head down and ran even faster. Amazingly, the boys discovered a spurt of extra speed. They were closing in on the stone head.

"Keep going, Rory," panted Cameron. He took advantage of his longer strides and overtook his brother. With concentration on his little face, Rory scrambled on. He gritted his teeth. His brown hair flopped as he ran. Their steps ate up the ground between them and the stone head.

Cameron made it to the stone head and kept his pace strong. He knew what was coming next. At least, he hoped that he knew. Just as before, it swallowed him whole and he passed out of the mezzanine. Daniel gasped to see his son collide with the stone column and disappear out of view. In theory, his boy had hit an immovable object at full speed. The laws of physics decreed that he should have bounced off as the kinetic energy was transferred back at him. But instead, he slipped in like a diver entering a pool.

Unfortunately, Rory wasn't so lucky. One of the demons split from the others and gained on him. Without any warning, he plucked him off the ground and took him high up into the air. His panic-stricken expression was the last thing they saw as his small but muscular legs kicked up and down.

Arabella screamed, "No, no, no!"

Satisfied with their prize, the demons whirled around and flew back in the direction they had come from. Arabella twirled round to do an about-face, looking at them all the while. She stared across the plain, watching them go. Her shoulders sank. Daniel took one final glance and then turned to stare at the stone head. He looked to see if Cameron would come back.

"What do we do?" screamed Arabella, desperately. "Daniel! What do we do?" She bent over double, racked with despair. A series of sobs overwhelmed her.

Daniel paused for a moment longer. Then, just as Caleb had taught him, he sat down on the ground and closed his eyes. It made perfect sense to him now. In the face of danger, in the midst of the storm, facing the impossible, he knew just what to do.

"Rescuer, we need your help. Dunamis, lead us," he whispered under his breath. "Creator, we are in your hands. Powerless."

"What are you doing? Are you going to do nothing?" Arabella shrieked.

Daniel opened his eyes. Perfectly calmly, he said to her, "I'm doing the only thing I know how to do with any certainty. I love you, Bella. Come here."

Arabella walked heavily over to her husband and put her arms around him. "Oh, Dan," she sobbed.

"Here's what we're going to do. You follow Cameron through the portal. Find him, look after him and stay with him until I come. Find somewhere obvious where I'll find you. Where we'll find you, me and Rory. I'll be as quick as I can. I'm going to get him."

"But you don't know where they've taken him." She started to cry again.

"He is going to be all right," he said, serenely. "I'll find him. I am confident he's going to be all right."

"I wish I could be so sure."

Chapter 15

"Go now, sweetie. I won't be long," said Daniel. He urged Arabella to go towards the stone head, trying to prevent an emotional goodbye. Clearly conflicted by the decision, she stood paralysed, staring at him.

"But, Rory…"

"I'll find him. Cameron needs you. Go on. And trust me."

With a deep frown and heavy steps Arabella got herself over to the giant head.

She glanced back at Daniel and said, "Bring him back quickly." Memories of a thousand partings flooded her mind. Saying goodbye to her parents at university. Abandoning the kids for the first time at playgroup. Leaving Daniel at an airport. Saying goodbye to him at a train station. Kissing him goodbye as he went to work in the morning. Watching him go on another trip at night. So many goodbyes – too many. Part of her wondered whether she would ever see Daniel again. Or her little boy – her baby.

Resignedly, she faced the stone head and forced her body through it, back to Earth. The cold surface accepted her. She passed through.

As soon as he was sure she had made the transition, Daniel turned and walked quickly back the way they had come. He was certain the creatures had taken his son to the caves. It was what they did to Caleb and his friends, Anton and Eli. They kept them prisoners and inflicted unspeakable torments on them.

"Rescuer, I could really do with meeting you now. I hear you have a nice horse. Do you fancy collecting me and taking me with you? Perhaps you can bust Rory out of captivity? If he's dead, maybe you can bring him back? Where are you, Rescuer?"

He walked quickly down the hill, finding the journey much easier without his family. Daniel stayed fit by using a basement room in Lytescote Manor as his private gym. He wasn't one to brag but he was very proficient on the rowing machine and often ran long distances on the treadmill.

The strange thing about the mezzanine was that fitness levels didn't seem to matter much. It was possible to walk immense distances without requiring any rest. Sleep was relatively pointless here. It probably served some sort of purpose but it wasn't the same as back on Earth. Also, he was never hungry or thirsty which was fine with him. Although he liked his food he could happily do without having to eat. That way, he would get more done, he reasoned.

Very soon he was back at the desolate landscape where the spider creatures had attacked their minds. It was still morning and he could see clearly, unlike before. He saw a wide flat surface, littered with rocks and holes.

He continued his one-way conversation with the Rescuer. "Yes, so if not a horse, then perhaps a couple of angels? Those black things could certainly fly very fast, but I'm sure your angels can match them for speed. How about it?"

Daniel flinched as a streak of chartreuse-coloured lightning flashed through the magenta sky. It hit the rocks to his right but they didn't explode. The thought that came into his mind was that he was standing in a meteor shower.

"I am Sarakiel," said a figure. He appeared to emerge from the lightning itself.

Daniel had seen all sorts of things in the demonic world in which he used to dwell. Sorcery and shape shifting, invisibility spells and levitation. Samyaza had fed him as much of the occult as he could eat. The problem was that the dark arts rotted the bones. Their source was demonic and so was their ultimate purpose. There was no good magic, Daniel discovered. When he met the Dunamis for the first time, he knew the source of his supernatural power was different. It was good. Pure. That was something the darknesss could never emulate.

He remembered sitting with Caleb and Eli on the boat. They invited the Dunamis to come and he had been filled with such sweet peace. Nothing Samyaza could generate would ever be so clean. So powerful. It was a light that could flush out any darkness. And that light was inside him now – a core part of him. He had gone from being darkness to light.

Everything about Sarakiel indicated that he was full of that light: the purity of the Dunamis. Daniel marvelled at his bright white robe. It flashed with lightning first of all and then settled down to being bright white. It was one of the few things that wasn't stained pale red-purple by the overarching sky. Even the water took on the hues from above.

He remembered meeting his first angel, Mattatron. He appeared to Rachel and his family down by the caves. But Mattatron hadn't come for him. No, it was Caleb he was after. He had flown away with him, only to return the man full of courage and boldness and with white hair to boot! It was like Caleb had received a version upgrade. Caleb two point zero.

Next time, Mattatron led Caleb away again when it was time to return to Griffton. That time, Caleb reappeared in Griffton with Serena. It seems that whenever he went off with the angels, something major happened. Perhaps this was Daniel's turn to have an adventure. That would be great, he thought. Particularly if it ended up with him holding his son in his arms. Alive.

He ventured to say, "You're a Warrior Angel. Did I summon you?"

"No, Daniel. We saw you walking through the valley. We were chasing the Angel Hunters. We saw them take your boy." His voice was deeper than most human voices. His tones were tinged with low white noise: edged with an almost imperceptible rumbling.

"A coincidence then?"

"I did not say that."

Daniel smiled wanly. "Do you know where they have taken him?"

"Yes. I will lead you there. I'd like to help. In fact, I was made to help."

"That's good news."

"Are you ready? Do not be afraid," he said comfortingly.

"I'm not afraid," said Daniel, but Sarakiel had taken hold of him with two strong arms. He propelled them both into the air with his colossal wings.

"Okay, now I am," bleated Daniel.

°°°°°*12345*°°°°°

Sarakiel set Daniel down by a stream. The familiar sound of trickling water filled his ears. There was a cave mouth nearby. It was a small and low opening and Daniel saw he would need to crouch to enter.

"Is Rory in there?"

Sarakiel nodded. Daniel tightened his backpack and stooped to look inside. All he could see was darkness. He reached for the right side of his bag and extracted his flashlight.

"Are you sure you can fit in that hole?"

In an instant, Sarakiel became a streak of lightning that shot through the cave mouth, illuminating the rocks inside. They glowed luminous green.

"I see," said Daniel, standing up.

Seconds later, the angel came back. Daniel imagined him bouncing on all the walls of the rock complex, leaving a trail of light as he went.

He transformed into an angelic being again. "There's a long passageway. You turn right, then left again into a large chamber. My comrades are there, battling the Angel Hunters. I must rejoin them without delay."

"Okay," noted Daniel. "Is Rory in there? Is it safe for me?"

"Yes he is. You can come but be careful. Seek the Rescuer for success. Human faith aids us immensely in our fight. Have hope – regardless of what you see in there. Come quickly now."

Again, Sarakiel became a streak of green-yellow light and projected himself into the cave. Daniel crouched down and followed on his hands and knees. He would have preferred to travel as a thread of light himself. It looked far easier.

He held his flashlight in his mouth, between his teeth. The beam bounced around, showing him a dry and dusty floor, seeded with rocks. He followed the angel's directions and went through a long shaft which met an intersection. Here, he was able to crouch and walk along with his back bent. By the time he got to the left hand turn, he was able to stand, though his hair brushed the ceiling.

Next the caves opened up and became a large cavern where he could stand and walk around freely. The roof was high above his head. The sound of his shuffling went out and came back to him like an army of beavers building a dam. And so did the sound of fighting.

Three white Warrior Angels fought three black Angel Hunter demons. Daniel entered but pressed his back to the wall furthest away from them. He had no intention of getting involved. Their strength and powers were clearly greater than his. Gingerly, he shone his light across them, looking for Rory. But he couldn't see him anywhere.

Remembering the angel's request, Daniel breathed deeply and called on the Rescuer. Under his breath, he said, "Rescuer, this battle is already won. I know it, and you know it. These foul creatures will lose. Your agents will beat them. It's a done deal. Come help us, mighty Rescuer."

He started off quietly, but quickly found that he was speaking loudly. Boldly. Confidently. Flashes of light came from the angels. Daniel directed his own light and his gaze directly at the enemy. Meanwhile, he willed the Warrior Angels to defeat their foe. In this confined space, their swords clashed against the talons and wings of the enemy. He saw, almost in freeze-frame, a set of piercing black eyes; a ruthless mouth; the flash of a blade, a line of dark blood.

One of the black creatures fell, gashed by the long edge of a broadsword. The angel finished him off, leaving his corpse behind: motionless. Daniel was unable to tell the angels apart, to see which one was his new friend Sarakiel.

Two angels converged on one of the nightmare creatures. Although he shrieked horribly, he too fell by the sword. He was unable to withstand the double attack. This left just one enemy.

"Come on!" Daniel shouted.

The demon froze and stared at him across the cave. Daniel felt the presence of evil. It was like the weight of Samyaza perching on his soul. The creature's gaze bore down on him, pinning him to the wall.

Suddenly, it flew at him, hatred in its eyes. It hissed and shrieked simultaneously, hurtling towards him. Daniel froze. But Sarakiel was there by his side. He had transported himself as a beam of chartreuse lightning and reassembled next to Daniel. In his hand was a long metal blade, fashioned for such a time as this. Unable to halt his course, the demon impaled himself on Sarakiel's sword with his momentum becoming his enemy. He collapsed onto the ground in a massive heap, dead. Daniel recoiled, but was thankful to be alive.

Silence filled the caves. The four of them enjoyed the long seconds of respite. The Warrior Angels cleaned their weapons and stood tall.

"Rory?" said Daniel urgently.

"We will go and search for him," said one of the angels in response.

"I saw him over there when I looked through the caves," Sarakiel told them. "But I had to leave him so we could fight."

Daniel looked horrified.

"It was necessary. Let them check on him." Sarakiel stayed with Daniel while the other two became streaks of lightning that shot away in different directions. They were back in a heartbeat.

"He is through here. Come quickly."

Daniel rushed through the next cave and then into the adjoining one. Sarakiel didn't leave his side.

Sitting at the foot of a hard rocky wall was his little six-year-old boy, Rory. His hands and face were pale. It was unclear whether or not he was breathing. Next to him was a translucent octopus with a gash in its head.

"I killed the Valenstriuccia as soon as I found it," said Sarakiel.

Daniel ran over to Rory and swept him up in his arms. A sudden wave of emotion came over him and he wept, pulling him close into his body. He knew what it meant to have one of these hideous creatures on your head. He had seen what Caleb had become. It was the last thing he wanted for his child.

"We have to get out of here," he said quietly. "Are you able to take us out?"

"No," said Sarakiel. "But we will stay with you."

This time, the angels didn't transform themselves into light beams. Instead, they walked with Daniel through the interconnected caves. Then they helped him to carry Rory out through the low and narrow channel. Eventually, they emerged into daylight.

Outside it was afternoon in the mezzanine. The clouds had cleared and the sky was a thrilling shade of violet. One of the angels put Rory down on the bank, resting his head on a grassy patch. He was groggy but alive. Daniel crouched by him and held his soft hand. No words came from Rory's mouth. He was unable to smile, which broke Daniel's heart.

"Human," remarked Sarakiel. He stood by Daniel's side.

"Yes," answered Daniel.

"No. There's a human. Over there."

Daniel looked up and saw Micah coming towards them. He was walking at a steady pace, and his almond-shaped eyes were blank.

"Hey Micah! Where are the others? Is Caleb okay? Did you find the door?"

Micah came closer. "I see the boy is hurt," he commented in a gravelly voice. "Let me take a look?"

Daniel was suddenly on his guard. "You're not Micah. You're him. Sarakiel! Help!"

All of a sudden Micah shape-shifted into Zed, the red-eyed, wispy-haired misanthrope. He had a crazed expression and a horrible mouth that housed an uncontrollable tongue. Daniel saw he was clutching a pointed knife in each hand.

Laughing maniacally, he unleashed a stunning and ferocious attack on Sarakiel. He brought his arms out wide and repeatedly plunged the blades into his sides, laughing all the while. They sank deep.

Sarakiel's wings twitched awkwardly. He let out a deep groan and collapsed to the ground.

The assault left the other two angels stunned. However, they instinctively found their weapons and ran forward to face the enemy. But Zed shape-shifted again. He quickly became a huge tiger, a beautiful black-striped creature that quickly bound away, snarling as it raced. It scampered across the rocks.

"Go," Sarakiel commanded, gasping. His companions clutched their swords and took to their wings. They chased the tiger along the bank of the stream. But it eluded them. It pranced and leapt, splashing up water with its paws. Seconds later Zed transformed himself once more. He sprang upwards and became a falcon. The bird soared into the air like a dart. It ascended rapidly, becoming a tiny dot on the horizon.

Desperately, Daniel watched as the angels changed into lightning streaks in order to catch him. He waited, peering into the sky. One of his hands was on Rory and the other was on Sarakiel's arm. He lost sight of both the lightning and the falcon.

Daniel dropped his head. He felt Rory starting to stir. But Sarakiel lay still. His life had departed.

Chapter 16

The route was not as straightforward as Caleb had hoped. The cave system was showing itself to be massive and complicated. As he tried to lead Serena and Micah, they were required to stop frequently to call on the Dunamis. It felt as though one wrong turn could take them in completely the wrong direction. The consequence of that could mean they would never find their way out. In turn, that meant they would never find and activate their Protector.

There were caves within caverns and narrow gaps you had to squeeze through. From time to time, they were surprised to find large pools of water, towering ceilings, unexpected columns and long corridors. Sometimes, they were forced to stop at a dead end and retrace their steps.

In their favour, all three of them were used to listening for the voice of the Dunamis. Caleb had developed his connection through the years, particularly latterly. During his wife Rosemary's illness, and during her last days and beyond, he lent on the Rescuer and his Dunamis. It was the only thing that kept him going: his support and his strength. A crutch for a weak man.

After she died, he went travelling. He grieved and healed, talking to the Dunamis all the while. Sometimes he sat and wept. He often asked questions that he could not find answers to. Once in a while he got an unexpected solution. Many nights he just lay and listened and relaxed in the presence of the King.

One day, he found he was stronger inside. He still missed Rosemary desperately. But his hope had returned. The Dunamis went from being a crutch for the weak to a sword for the strong. Battles continued to rage because life is struggle: with the Rescuer King by his side, he lived a triumphant life, the life of an overcomer.

As for Serena, she had always experienced a very strong and clear sense of the Dunamis' leading. Ever since she was a child. Her parents followed the Rescuer in secret at a time when opposition was at its height. They were living in America but the book burnings were the decider for them. They felt they had to leave and go far away.

They relocated to a remote Indonesian island and taught her their way: the way of faith. That was when she discovered her prophetic gift. The Dunamis told her things about people and about things that would happen through the hazy window of the future. He also gave her encouraging words for them that would give them hope.

For some of the people she came into contact with, this was liberating. It meant they knew there was a Creator who cared about them and knew everything about them. A friend of hers, a young boy from the village, contracted a skin disease. The Dunamis told her he would heal him if she was obedient. She had to tell him there is a Creator who would make his skin pure again because he loves him.

Serena cried when the Dunamis asked her to do this. She was scared of rejection. Scared of being labelled a freak. But she didn't want his voice to go away so, with her heart in her mouth, she told her friend. The boy was healed and believed. It was all they could do to keep it quiet.

For others her gift was a threat. Three times, overzealous neighbours reported her family to the authorities. They were forced to move on or face arrest. She learned to be more circumspect.

One day, her parents were murdered. It wasn't actually her gift or her carelessness that resulted in the death of her parents. They were caught with a partial copy of an illegal book. Horrified that it had escaped the book burning, the authorities seized it by force and her parents were killed in the arrest. It was written up as an accident, but Serena, who was twenty-six at the time, knew the truth. She fled to Bali, which became her home from that time.

The Rescuer kept her single throughout her life, until she was forty-two. This was often a sadness to her. She had good friends and enjoyed her own company. But she often remonstrated with him and asked him to send her a soul mate.

When she met Caleb in Bali, she knew why he had done this. He had set her apart for him. While she was single, his wife Rosemary was still alive. It would not have worked. Now he was free and so was she. They found each other by chance, which was, in fact, design. It was not something she could have arranged herself. And now she had a ring on her finger and her husband Caleb by her side. Her joy was complete.

"So, where did you guys meet?" Micah asked. They were walking through a spherical chamber the size of a cathedral. Caleb's powerful flashlight lit the way, revealing smooth, curved walls.

Serena laughed, a light and girlish laugh. "Would you believe we met in Indonesia?"

"I could believe that," said Micah.

"Well, we met in Indonesia. It was last year. The Initiation had occurred and Caleb was looking for answers. He found me in Bali. I live near Kuta Beach in the south. Do you know it?"

"Not really. Is it near Manilla?"

"No. That's the Philippines," Caleb interrupted.

"Oh. Okay then. So, you got married?"

"We certainly did. Have you ever been in love, Micah?" Serena asked him.

"Not really."

"Not really?"

Serena saw Micah blush in the artificial white light. "Don't look so serious. I'm just having fun with you, she smiled." While they walked, the Dunamis told her about Micah.

He had been in love once. He was living somewhere else at the time. In the North of England. He wasn't with Daniel and Arabella then. That happened later. He was younger, fourteen. It was a girl. He loved her and she toyed with him over a long period of time. Then she went off with his best friend.

The reason the rejection and betrayal wounded his heart so much was he was thirsty for love. Being orphaned, he had been robbed of his parents' love. He'd built a shell to protect his heart, and was only now starting to heal. The Rescuer was helping him to heal. But sometimes these things take time.

"Sorry Micah," she smiled, sympathetically. But she didn't tell him what she was sorry for.

°°°°°12345°°°°°

They emerged into daylight. Caleb emitted a booming laugh and switched off his flashlight. He was happy to hook it back on his belt.

"We made it."

Caleb had been apprehensive about the caves and, on entering them, had felt an impending sense of dread. It was a place of horror: the place where he had been tortured and his two best friends had been killed. It had also become their tomb, a thought that stayed with him as he ventured through the darkness.

However, in this dank, echoing place, the Rescuer gave him strength to persevere. He also leaned on his long years of experience, trusting the Creator who saw the bigger picture. He was certain he would be reunited with his friends again.

Serena put her arm around him and gave his shoulder a squeeze. In the distance was a broad lake. On top of the surrounding hills, Caleb could see intricate tiers of rock. They were reminiscent of pale coral. From a distance they could be mistaken for an elaborate city whose walls were chiselled and carved by the finest craftsmen. Caleb imagined it as an angelic city: the place where the angel army lived.

"Does anyone like sailing?" asked Serena suddenly. "The Dunamis says we need to cross that lake. We'll find our doorway on the other side."

"Can we go around it?" Micah enquired.

"No. We need to go over it."

"Why?"

"Danger," explained Serena, widening her green eyes.

"Oh, okay."

"In that case, we need to look for a boat," Caleb declared. "Let's go and see what we can find."

The ground outside the caves was dusty and red. It led downhill to the shore of the lake. They couldn't see any decent paths along the side of the water. It was possible to walk a little way, but then it became difficult to continue. There were thickets and spiky weeds in the way. Going back away from the lake the ground became rocky and impassable.

They stood by the water and stared. "I can't see anything," Micah complained.

Suddenly, Caleb's face lit up.

"What do you see? Can you see a boat?" Micah asked excitedly.

"Not exactly. What do you reckon about those tall plants over there? Don't they look a bit like bamboo?"

"What do you mean?"

"I've got a knife and some string. Have you ever made a raft?"

Micah stared at Caleb as though he were mad. "That isn't something I've ever done. Have you?"

"No. But how hard can it be?" Caleb smiled, revealing a neat line of teeth.

"Ever thought to ask me?" Serena asked seriously.

"Why? Do you know about rafts?"

"Does your wife know about rafts? I've pretty much lived my whole life on one island or another. How do you think we pass the time? We eat amazing seafood and mess about in the water.

You guys are so fortunate to have me with you."

"I love you even more each day," said Caleb.

"You so do."

Micah rolled his eyes.

"Okay then. Let's get to work."

It took them a couple of hours to cut down the poles and line them up. Then, it took a considerable amount of time to lash them together with Caleb's string. The raft needed to carry three of them across the water. So it needed to be big. Serena had been used to building smaller rafts for one or two people. Nevertheless, she applied herself to the task and expertly carved wood to make simple joints and tied dozens of knots. Caleb seemed to have an endless supply of string which was fortunate.

By the time they finished the work it was night-time. He decided it was too dangerous to set out, particularly if they couldn't see where they were going.

Their minds told them they should be tired by the exertion. Nobody felt tired though. They were, instead, excited about the prospect of crossing the river. Caleb in particular was really looking forward to it. He loved sailing, and recalled times when he had been on the water with Anton and Eli.

They settled down on the bank beside the raft.

Despite protesting that he would stay awake the whole night, Micah fell asleep.

"It's a little bit like having a teenage son," said Serena.

"An older teenage son," Caleb commented.

"Yes, a nineteen-year-old. That's how old he is, isn't he?"

"I think so. It means that, if he was our son, you and I would have been married close to his age. Not far off."

Serena laughed. "I remember being that age once. We were living in the Indonesian island of Flores at the time. My parents were still alive," she said sadly. He put his hand on hers.

Then they heard a strange sound coming over the water. It was the low hiss of white noise, broken up with jagged silences. The rattlesnake noise rose in a crescendo. It ended with a loud gasp.

Then silence. This happened several times.

Serena looked at Caleb. "What do you think that is?"

Caleb shook his head. They stared across the lake. All they could see was water, stretching for miles. The water was stained dark red by the night sky. There was nothing poking out. Nothing approached them.

"We should seek the Dunamis together," he said. "And also for Rachel's protection. And the Harcourts."

Serena was in agreement and so they shut their eyes and asked the Rescuer to protect their friends wherever they were. Peace descended on them. They pictured Rachel, Eddie and Lake, resting for the night. Then they envisaged Daniel and Arabella with Rory and Cameron. Everyone was alive and unharmed, they felt. The mission was on track.

Caleb opened his eyes and looked across the lake. The hissing sound came back at him, rising to a peak and finishing with a gasp. He held Serena closer and stayed vigilant.

Chapter 17

Micah sat squarely on the raft and dug the oar into the water. It was made of a half section of bamboo pole, or whatever passes as bamboo in the mezzanine. It did the trick though. The water made a satisfying swishing sound as he pushed through it. He lifted his stick back out and jabbed it in the lake once again. A breeze stroked his face. It offered him satisfying proof that they were moving forwards. All the while, he tried to keep his balance and not fall headfirst into the water.

They were indeed shifting ahead at a reasonable pace. Serena and Caleb lay at the front of the raft on their fronts and paddled with their hands. They preferred to do this, even though Micah thought an oar would be more effective.

Serena had helped them to assemble a great raft. It was long and wide, perfect for transporting the three of them. He admitted to himself that he didn't think she could do it at first. But the three of them had got to work and the result was impressive. It even held together, which was a feat in itself. So, with great excitement, they pushed off into the water. And that was where they were now, a quarter of the way across the lake.

It was a sizeable lake but not so big you couldn't see the edges. It was an oval-shaped body of water. Black rocks rose on the right side. Red and purple plants edged the other shore to the left. In the distance in front of them was the far shore where they were headed.

They could see the structures on the high hills more clearly now. The rocks were lined with a complex arrangement of horizontal ridges. They looked like they were made of coral: both delicate and robust at the same time. The colours were notable. Pale pinks and purples swirled into each other and the higher ridges had aquamarine streaks. They could now see tiny red rocks floating in the sky above the structures.

They paddled for most of the day without stopping. But some time in the afternoon, they all sat and rested, not that their bodies needed to. They kept the raft on course by paddling with their hands periodically. Serena was keen to ensure they travelled in a straight line. She checked with the others that the right and left banks were still the same distance away as when they started.

"I think we need to steer right now. We're going off course!" she cried. The men obliged and got them back on track.

Caleb saw a bird fly into the clouds above. It circled quickly and descended. As it came closer to them, he saw it was a falcon.

"Hey! I know that bird," Caleb exclaimed.

"What? You know that exact bird?" Micah said wryly.

"I know it's a falcon. My friend Anton had one. He kept one in a cage in his shed. He lived in Scotland," he added, as though that explained everything.

Micah smiled at him.

Unexpectedly the bird flew down towards them at a steep angle. It circled around and approached from behind the raft. Incredibly, the falcon, a brown and blue bird with a yellow beak, landed right on the back of the vessel. It had quick, beady eyes and fluttered its feathers twitchily.

"Watch out!" Caleb shouted to Micah, sensing danger.

"It's just a bird," said Micah.

The falcon quickly shape-shifted into a man. It went from having a tiny body to being a full-sized person. It was like watching a fruit ripen in time-lapse photography. First it was little, and then it was fully grown and bulbous. It grew into a young man. Micah found himself looking at a perfect copy of himself.

"Ugh!" he said, gawking at his nemesis. Everything about the creature was identical to him. He saw his wide jaw, dark wavy hair and almond-shaped eyes. The body was slim and sporty. It was him. Except he knew that he was him. It was confusing.

"Look at your face," laughed the other Micah. Then he pushed him ferociously into the water. Micah felt like he'd been hit with a slab of concrete. He went over sideways and plunged headfirst into the lake.

"By the power of the Dunamis," roared Caleb, rearing up, "I rebuke you!" Refusing to be intimidated, he started to move towards the creature.

Serena shrank back, seeing the fake Micah produce two thin blades. They glinted in the mezzanine sun. Micah shape shifted again and became his real self: Zed the craftsman. Zed the murderer. There was something horrible about his mouth, thought Serena. It was crooked. His teeth were discoloured and yellow: broken-down tombstones. And his tongue appeared to have a mind of its own, slithering around in his mouth. She shivered.

He locked his red eyes onto her, bringing himself up to his full height. Caleb watched him carefully, ready to act. Then Zed lunged at them. One knife was meant for her and the other for him. It was a double attack.

"Time to join your friends," spat Zed.

Micah popped up at the back of the raft. He sputtered and splashed in the water. His long hair was dripping as he shook his head. He kicked his legs and grabbed for the raft. Both of his hands landed on the surface.

"Micah!" screamed Serena.

He pushed down hard in order to rock the whole structure. It see-sawed. Not expecting this at all, Zed lost his balance. Caleb grabbed his advantage. He unhooked his flashlight from his belt with his right hand. Then, calling for help from the Dunamis, he beat it down hard on Zed's left wrist. It made a gratifying cracking sound. The strike made him drop one of his knives. The one meant for Serena. The weapon skidded off the raft and into the water.

Zed started to shape shift again. This time, Caleb jabbed his heavy flashlight into his temple. Zed failed to execute his manoeuvre. Stunned for a moment, it left him open to attack.

Caleb's thoughts were crystal clear. Protect his friends. Stop Zed. Revenge was not his main driver, though it should be. After all, this vile body of vomit had killed his two best friends. No, staying alive and activating the Protector was his primary aim. If saving the human race was not motivation enough, then nothing would be. And this creature was in the way of his objective.

He growled and threw himself forcefully at the attacker. The hunted became the hunter.

Zed's face contorted with rage. He snarled, uttering a disturbing sound from the back of his throat. Caleb, muscular and fast, fell on top of him. He pounded him on the side of his head. He was still mindful of the knife though. So, when Zed tried to stab him in the right side, he pressed his arm down hard with his own. Zed's wrist was pinned to the raft by Caleb's strong forearm.

The enemy mustered superhuman strength. He rolled his body to the edge of the raft. The force pushed both Zed and Caleb into the water. Only Serena was left on the raft. Micah still held onto the back, treading water.

Underwater, Caleb and Zed wrestled. Water splashed up around the others. Serena peered over, willing Caleb to win. She closed her eyes and called on the Dunamis to protect her husband and save them all. The fight lasted for several minutes but it seemed much longer to her. Serena and Micah waited anxiously, unable to tell what was going on. Micah was in two minds about diving down and helping Caleb. He didn't trust his swimming abilities and thought he would be more of a hindrance than a help.

Suddenly it was over. Zed's body was the first to materialise. It popped up next to the raft. The blade stuck out of his chest at right angles. Micah took a sharp intake of breath. Then he relaxed, realising it was over. Zed's red-rimmed eyes stared crazily at the purple sky but saw nothing. Zaelaza's time in the mezzanine was over.

Caleb swam up to the surface and threw his head back as he emerged. Water ran off his closely-cropped head. He placed his muscular arms on the raft and breathed heavily.

"Everyone okay?" he called out.

"Yes! We're all okay. Are you?"

"He bit me. Can you imagine it? He bit me on the arm. The animal," Caleb complained. "Apart from that, I'm fine. I'm alive."

Caleb only wanted to rest briefly. He felt a real urgency to get to the stone head. So he insisted they continue paddling until they got to dry land. Everyone was in agreement, so they pulled together and made good time across the rest of the lake. They abandoned Zed's body far behind: food for the pterodactyls.

On the other side, they found red soil, cluttered with purple shrubs and roots. They left the raft at the water's edge and put their packs on their backs. Silently, they walked uphill. The ground rose away from the lake. The shrubs grew taller and black trees started to appear. A forest sprang up. Broad branches sheltered them from the sun. They walked on.

Their path began to plateau. The trees grew more sparse and the landscape changed. They discovered an open plain. The ground was dry, comprising dark red dust and hardy scrub. Black boulders and tall monoliths lived here. They sat on the ground like huge knuckles. A solitary tree squatted in the midst of them with black bark and gnarly branches. Wind blew across the desert land.

Micah spotted the stone head far away. Standing in the middle of nowhere, the prehistoric face was turned towards them. Tiny in the distance, it waited patiently for them to come.

"It's over there. That's our door. It has to be," he said quietly.

Serena nodded. "Yes, that's it all right."

"We're nearly there," Caleb agreed. He scanned the horizon for enemies. The coast was clear. "Let's do it," he said.

It took a while, but they successfully crossed the desert without any further surprises. They had grown accustomed to the stone heads. Caleb had mixed feelings about them. He had been thrown through one in Bolivia before being imprisoned in the mezzanine. He'd walked willingly through another with his new wife Serena. That was the one on Griffton Cliff. He had returned to that head on this current adventure.

The heads were, perhaps, not evil in themselves, though he understood they had come out of the vortex after the Initiation. He also knew they sent a surge of electricity out to prevent the wrong people from going through. Sometimes they lay dormant, refusing passage. They were also used by the Dream Fighters to cross the globe.

But they could also be harnessed for good. The angels had encouraged them to use them to get to the destinations. They opened up the way to connect with the angelic army and the Rescuer. It was like so many things that existed. They could be used for good or bad purposes.

So here they were. Standing before the unhappy-looking stone face with its deep-set eyes and long mouth. Like the others, it towered above them ten feet in the air: a wall of thick grey rock.

"Shall we?" asked Caleb. He took one last look behind him. The desert plain was clear of danger. Rough, dry ground spread out for miles in every direction. The sky was clear of birds or demons.

While he scanned the horizon, Serena punched him on the arm and said, "Come on, you slow coaches."

She was the first one to go through the portal. He turned to see half her body disappear.

"Hey! Wait for me," he snapped.

Micah laughed and went in after her. Being used to leading, rather than following, Caleb knitted his brow and frowned.

"Oh, all right then," he grumbled. But there was no one left to listen to him. "Here we go, on to the end of the world," he said. And then he skipped through the stone head.

Chapter 18

The Grigori and their Nephilim moved leisurely through Uzbekistan. They carried on west through Turkmenistan. They didn't respect borders. If they met an immovable object, such as a barrier, a wall or border control, they smashed through it. Nothing hindered or prevented their advance.

Behind them, a sand storm raged across the desert lands. Grey dust, black smoke and powdered buildings mingled with the sand. The dirty mixture filled the air, borne aloft on the winds. Explosions hollowed out the landscape. These particular lands were rich in gas resources. The enemy was delighted to discover this. Random explosions added to the mayhem they could create.

Turkmenistan was a controlling and brutal nation. But it met its match when the invaders arrived. The attackers crushed this nation's red, rectangular desert houses to dust. They broke the bodies of their villagers and abandoned them far away from home. Just as a cat selects a bird at random to toy with, in such a way did the enemy mess with the people they encountered.

Before they died, the people saw, perhaps, a shadow on a wall, or a huge black wing. Others saw dead eyes gazing at them up close, or the flash of a blade. Random and brutal was the attack which came like a thief in the night. It left the survivors paralysed, unable to function. Satisfied, the demonic marauders left them in that state.

They paused briefly by the coastal waters before swimming the

Caspian Sea: the world's largest lake. Only then did their feast of destruction come to a halt. The dark figures floated in the deep water. Their bare heads bobbed up and down like buoys marking out dangerous waters. Only one Grigori flew the distance. It was the huge fallen angel, Samyaza. Disfigured and grotesque, he beat his wings slowly. He glided back and forth proudly over the heads of his army.

Triumphant in victory, Samyaza soared upwards towards the moon, bathed in its chalky glow. He bared his razor-sharp teeth and hissed. His gums were wet with the blood of the last human he'd feasted on.

Azerbaijan lay unsuspecting over the waters.

°°°°°12345°°°°°

As they looked at the river which ran under the rocks, Lake started to laugh.

"What's so funny, Lake?" sighed Rachel. Eddie was looking unsuccessfully for handholds in the cliff. He twisted his neck round to regard them, eyebrows raised.

"I think I might have heard from him. Me. Imagine!"

"The Dunamis?"

"I know!"

"So, what's he saying?"

"Swim. He's saying we need to jump in the river and swim."

"But we'll hit our heads on that rock. What exactly did he say?"

"He said: jump in the river and swim."

"Anything else? What's on the other side?"

"Well, I think he showed me a sort of movie of us swimming. It played in my head. We dive into the water and swim under the rock. In the film, we make it through to the other side."

"And you're sure it's him?"

Lake shrugged. "I'm pretty sure. Not that I've ever heard him before. But I don't think I made it up. I mean, it sounds like a fun thing to do and it does make sense. Kinda."

139

"Dad, what do you think?"

Eddie looked serious. He squinted at Lake. Then he nodded.

"Follow the river. That's what Serena got. Jump in and swim. It sounds like it might be him," said Eddie.

Lake looked delighted. "He spoke to me," he said proudly.

"It's exciting," Rachel agreed. "We're all good swimmers. I've been in the waters here in the mezzanine before. The Rescuer will be with us. He loves water. He made me a special pool, you know."

"Rachel's Pool," Lake commented.

"Rachel's Pool," echoed Rachel.

She thought about all the times she'd jumped into the water. Being a Griffton girl, she'd been a swimmer all her life. They were used to being in the sea. Growing up, if they went anywhere decent on holiday, they'd try to find a lake to jump in. She loved the feeling of being surrounded by water. The front crawl was her best stroke, and she was faster and stronger than she looked. The prospect of jumping into this river, however, was both exhilarating and terrifying. She'd never done a bungee jump, but expected it felt much like this.

"Here's what we should do. Tighten your packs on your back. Make sure you don't have anything loose. Tie your coats around you. Let's jump in, get under that rock, and swim as hard as we can. If Lake's heard the King through the Dunamis, we'll be absolutely fine."

Lake smiled.

"If not, we're dead," Eddie added. Lake's face fell.

"I did hear him," he insisted.

"Boy, I believe you did," grinned Eddie. "Let's do this. I'm happy to go first. Leave space between us. Me, then Rach, then you, Lake. See you on the other side, and the Rescuer be with you."

°°°°°*12345*°°°°°

140

Kumiko arrived in convoy with the Dream Fighters at 42 Russet Road. She roared in on her motorbike. Her men brought an armoured car. It was their first assignment of the morning. They had many more to complete before the day was done. It didn't particularly bother them that their boss was with them on this one. They had a job to do and that was all there was to it.

With the air of a bureaucrat carrying out the task in hand, they got to work. Calmly, they climbed out of their armoured vehicle. Two soldiers arranged the petrol cans on the pavement. Meanwhile, two more went to the front door. They had a close look at it and decided not to kick it open. Instead, they moved over to the windows outside the front room. One produced a small metal battering ram. He used this to gain access to the house.

Kumiko watched eagerly from the street. She clapped her hands with glee, craning her neck to get the best view. Part of her hoped that Rachel was at home, sleeping in. That way she'd be burned alive. She wanted the father to be there too. Her remit included causing them harm if found.

One man climbed through the window. He appeared at the front door seconds later. Once inside, the Dream Fighters kicked over some chairs for the enjoyment of it. Upstairs, one of them smashed Rachel's guitar against the wall on Kumiko's request. They also stole a few items for themselves. One of them got Eddie's watch. The other snatched a chain.

Then they got to work preparing the place for destruction. They worked slowly and methodically. They tried to choose things that would ignite well, for maximum damage. Outside, Kumiko was getting restless, calling under her breath, "Come on. Come on." She clicked her nails on the roof of the car, willing the house to explode by narrowing her catlike eyes.

Once it was adequately doused with petrol, they lit the place up and left through the front door. The stench of chemicals and burning materials hit the street. It took a while for the flames to become visible though. Once they appeared, everyone seemed happier. It was a sunny morning, which made it all the more pleasant.

Kumiko sang and twirled as her men burned Rachel's house down. She sang with delight, warbling out of tune. She asked them, "Is she in there?"

Her man shook his head.

"No? That's a shame. Not to worry. We'll get her. But did you break something personal of hers? What did you find?"

"Her guitar, Master," answered one of the warriors.

"Oh that is good. That's excellent. I like it."

The warrior who'd spoken to her nodded and got into the car.

"He's coming. He's coming soon and then we'll really have some fun," Kumiko told him. "Sammy. Soon."

She turned to look at Rachel's house. It was full of fire. The flames danced and jumped, belching out dirty black smoke. She realised the houses on either side were likely to burn as well. It was the nature of terraced housing.

"Hey Rachel. Samyaza tells me you let him down. And you stole Lake away from me. It all comes at a price," she told the house.

Then she added, "Come home soon. I dare you."

°°°°°12345°°°°°

Rachel felt excited just before she jumped in. The cold water served to heighten this feeling. She felt alive and hyper-aware of everything, particularly the sensation of the icy water on her skin. The river had a strong current. Fortunately it didn't dash her carcass on the rocks at the bottom of the river. She assumed there were sharp rocks on the bottom. Instead, it carried her along quickly and efficiently like an airport walkway.

Eddie was in front of her and Lake behind. That was the order they chose. They spaced themselves well so they didn't kick each other in the head. She concentrated on keeping her head low. At the same time, she used her arms to propel herself forwards. It quickly grew dark. She fought her desire to panic.

The underwater swim seemed endless. Rachel realised there was little space between the river and the rock above. So she kept her body tucked neatly under the ceiling created by the cliff that stretched over her head.

She wondered how Lake was doing. She had enjoyed his company as they travelled. He made his silly jokes and childlike comments about everything he saw. But part of her loved this. He had a silliness and innocence that melted her. She also liked his sparkling eyes and his handsome smile.

Like her, he was an excellent swimmer. She gathered he had won lots of medals at school. He swam, he rollerbladed and he liked running and the gym. It kept him fit, she mused. It meant he had strong muscles and a lean body. She felt her heart swell as she thought of him. If everything turned out all right, she decided she would let him into her life again.

Red sunlight flooded the water. She looked up and saw the surface of the river. It was over. The top of her head broke through and she struggled for breath. She heard the sound of her dad's explosive wheezing. But she couldn't see Lake anywhere. The current dragged them downstream, unwilling to let go of them. She turned in the water, searching.

The cruel overhanging cliff receded into the distance. There were thick roots on the right-hand side of the river. Eddie grabbed one and started to haul himself onto the bank. He collapsed onto his front, breathing heavily, preoccupied by his own recovery.

Rachel kicked hard and sent herself towards the roots. As she grabbed them, Lake popped up, gasping for air. He was right by her.

"What a ride!" He managed before spluttering and gasping again.

"Lake! You idiot. Why did you stay down for so long? I was worried!"

"There's something you need to know about me, Rachel."

"Oh yeah, what's that?"

"I am fit."

"Fit, are you?"

"And don't you forget it."

Lake hauled himself up onto the bank next to Eddie. He reached out a hand for Rachel who was holding onto the root and treading water.

"Enjoy your swim?" he asked her.

"Hurry up and pull me out, Sportacus," she snapped. "Mister super-fit."

They wrung out their clothes and steeled themselves for the unpleasant experience of walking in damp apparel. However, they found it a lot easier to walk alongside the river again. There were no more jagged rocks. In their place was a pleasant mossy bank that was springy underfoot. Lime green and yellow flowers reclined on the riverbank. Above them stretched a purple sky devoid of clouds. The rays of the strange red sun warmed them. It even began to dry their clothes as they travelled.

Somewhere along the way, Rachel felt they were being followed. She whispered this to Eddie and then to Lake. Every so often, they peeked behind them. They couldn't see anything though.

And then they saw him in the distance. They paused to observe him properly. It was Olm, Zed's albino boy. He was standing as bold as a panther on the path behind them. The child wore a shabby T-shirt and long trousers that overhung his bare feet. His arms hung limp by his sides. Two hard lumps of coal stared at them and a black lizard tongue slid lazily across his lips. His balloon head sat upright on a lolly-stick neck. There was no sign of emotion in him.

"Do you know him?" Lake asked.

"Yeah, I know him," said Rachel quietly.

"Me too," hissed Eddie. "This creature is a vile monster. He comes straight from the darkness."

"Should we run?"

"Yeah. But watch out. He's different," Eddie warned. As they all watched Olm, his nature became apparent.

Lake opened his mouth and stared. The small albino boy was spawning into two people. The second one came out of the first and stepped aside. These two became half a dozen. Then there was a score of small albino boys. Very soon, the riverbank was overrun by lookalikes. They stood and looked coolly at the three mezzanine visitors.

Both Rachel and Eddie knew that any minute the herd of boys would charge them into oblivion.

"Get ready to run," Rachel said firmly.

Chapter 19

The groaning was almost unbearable. Daniel plodded on with Rory in his arms. He felt like he'd walked the length of the mezzanine. Mournful cries came from his son's mouth. They were high and woeful as the boy stared at untold horrors in his head.

"It's all right, Rory. It's okay. It's over. You're safe," Daniel insisted. But his words had no apparent effect.

His son was neither fully awake nor entirely asleep but appeared to be in an endless dream. Or perhaps he was in the space where dreams and wakefulness reside, thought Daniel. The beast that had sat on him was now dead though, he reasoned. So should he really still be in this state?

Daniel placed him down on the ground once again. The boy rolled onto his side and hugged his body. He carried on moaning. Daniel sat by him, staring across the plain. He stroked his head distractedly.

Memories flitted across his mind of all the times he'd been absent or walked away while the boys were growing up. There had always been something to do. A security project to oversee. A business deal to manage. And contracts and plans always seemed to have so many facets. The work took time. You had to wrestle with it to land it, or make sure it was done correctly. But do kids understand that?

When he wasn't making money, Samyaza gave him criminal activity to mastermind. There were people to extort, torture and manipulate. And, if he were honest with himself, there were hours that he grabbed for himself. He liked to read. He liked to think and listen to music. So, he locked himself away in his study or his downtown office. He had a full life. He needed his 'me-time'.

He didn't give a thought to Arabella and her requirements. He was providing them with money, so wasn't that enough? He certainly didn't think about the boys. He never considered figuring them into his plans. They were minors. Why should he make time for them? More often than not they just got in the way of what he needed to do. Wanted to do. Chose to do.

Now, it lay heavy on him. There was seemingly nothing he could do to help little Rory. Now was the time when Rory needed him the most. He was helpless.

Also on his mind was the angel. He had seen an angel die. A creature full of light and power. How could that be right? Angels were eternal beings, not ones who could be slain by demons. Surely? But he had seen his new champion, Sarakiel, lying lifeless next to him. If even the angels could be harmed in this mezzanine place, what hope was there for him or his son? How could they defend themselves?

He gasped and looked around quickly. There were so many places for predators to hide in this rocky scrubland. He checked the sky, the vast and perilous sky. It seemed to be flecked with black creatures. What if the demons came back? Samyaza already hated him for betraying him and siding with the Rescuer. The creatures in this world were darker and fiercer than anything he had encountered whilst working for Samyaza. They would rip him apart in an instant. Without an angel to protect him, one of those creatures could fly at him and destroy him within seconds. It almost happened in the cave. He shuddered.

Mixed in with his fear was an anger that rose up in him gradually and resolutely. How dare the evil ones do this to his son? He was furious that they had violated his boy's mind and put him into this coma of depression. He was angry with himself that he couldn't protect Rory better. And where were the angels?

If they can appear out of nowhere, why can't they come now? Why wasn't the Rescuer protecting him? Surely that was his job: to rescue and protect? What was the point of following a powerless king?

He scooped up his son and continued to walk across the rocky ground. Rory was heavier this time. After a dozen steps, the boy drifted out of his sleep and indicated that he wanted to stand. Daniel allowed him to do this.

"Hey fella. So, you've decided to join the living?"

But Rory was lost in his thoughts and couldn't find the way out. Still moaning, he stumbled hand-in-hand with Daniel, staring into infinity. Every so often Daniel's strong arm pulled him up, away from the gaps in the ground. Eventually, they climbed the hill that led to the stone head.

Quietly they passed through the doorway that led out of the mezzanine and onto Midway Island.

°°°°°12345°°°°°

Midway Island is a heart-shaped coral reef around two and a half miles square near Hawaii, in the North Pacific Ocean. The atoll is roughly equidistant between North America and Asia, and halfway around the world from Britain. It has three parts: Sand Island, Eastern Island – which is the smaller of the two – and the diminutive Spit Island between them.

With his head full of mezzanine purple, Daniel stepped into brilliant white sunlight. He was on Eastern Island, surrounded by bright blue ocean water. Hundreds of white and brown seabirds surrounded him. They chatted noisily, clacking and screeching to each other. He was also surrounded by the relentless hiss of waves moving against a beach and retreating.

Sea breeze blew into his face. Strong salty sea air invaded his lungs along with the stench of birds. It started to sink in: he was back on Earth. He was home.

He scanned the low-lying landscape, looking for the rest of his family. Rory sat back against a rock. Daniel turned around slowly in a full circle to take in the panorama. The place was full of leafy green bushes and thin brown grass, flecked with large yellow flowers and tiny white ones. Driftwood was strewn around the beach. The trunk of a dead tree poked upwards. Its barkless base was etched with vertical black lines and its mangled roots were exposed.

He flinched as a pair of angular black wings flew into his peripheral vision. But it was a sea bird, not a demon. It flew on and landed in a sandy patch of ground, away in the distance.

He relaxed. There were several mounds of sand near him. In the distance squat, luscious trees moved gently in the breeze. Beyond them was a strip of white foamy water, with a thick band of light-blue seawater behind it. Across the water, over to one side, was another island, covered in sand and bushes.

"Dad," called an excited voice. Cameron rose up from behind one of the sandy mounds and ran towards him. Arabella was with him. They both came quickly towards Daniel and Rory, leaping over the green clumps of vegetation.

Very soon, the four of them were hugging and chattering with the stone head towering over them. They thanked Daniel repeatedly for rescuing Rory but Arabella noticed quickly that he wasn't very responsive. "Is he okay?"

"They put one of those things on his head. Like Caleb."

"I see."

Suddenly, Cameron said, "Oh, he's going to be fine. Have you asked the Rescuer to bring him back, Dad?"

"What you mean?"

"You know. The power of the Dunamis that's in you. It can bring him back."

Daniel looked like someone had slapped him across the face. "You are right, Cam. No, I didn't do that. I should have done it straightaway but I didn't. Instead, I got angry and I stayed angry, but that's no good is it? We should do what you suggested right now! You can start us off."

"You mean me? Okay then!" Cameron sat down beside Rory. He put his arm around his brother and closed his eyes. Then he said, "Rescuer, my friend, bring back my brother Rory? They took him away and did bad things to his head, but I believe you can make him better again."

"Yes," Daniel added. "In the power of the Dunamis, Rory be healed."

They all peered at Rory. He opened his eyes wide. Arabella jerked back, surprised.

"Wow, an island. Are those all birds? Can we go for a swim? Why is it so hot?" chatted Rory.

Daniel pulled him close and wept silently into his hair.

°°°°°12345°°°°°

They worked out quickly that there was very little happening here on this island. Apart from the birds and the stone head, there was nothing of significant interest. There were three long aircraft landing strips and a couple of disused jetties that jutted into the sea. There was certainly no sign of any Sea Protector. Daniel and Arabella agreed to check out the other islands.

Conveniently, they were spotted by the local inhabitants on Sand Island. The Harcourt family approached the sandy shore just as a small white speedboat landed on the beach.

Daniel found himself shaking hands with a tall Japanese man called Judah. He wore a bright yellow Hawaiian shirt and sporty sunglasses. The man was a similar age to Daniel, perhaps slightly younger. His wife, Hannah, was African-American with a broad forehead and a wide smile. They seemed like nice, intelligent people, thought Daniel.

Their young son Stephen was all fringe and no face but the kids saw generous white teeth grinning at them and were put at ease. Stephen had coconut brown skin and was full of life. He wore a dark blue baseball cap to keep the sun off his black hair. He greeted the children warmly, and shook the hands of the adults.

"We knew you would come," said Judah in a deep and comforting voice. "The Dunamis told us, and so we are ready."

"We? The three of you?" Daniel checked.

"Ah, no. There are more. Come with us, we will feed you. You are hungry?"

Daniel looked at Arabella and she nodded. "You know what? I think we are probably all famished."

"Good news!"

"Do you know about the Protector?"

"All in good time, my friend," grinned Judah. "First, come and meet my people."

The boat took them the short hop between the two big islands, passing around the top of Spit Island. This was a triangular island consisting of sand and low green vegetation. The lagoon was calm and it was a pleasant trip. They crossed from the shadows of Spit Island into a deeper passage and then entered the shallows around the other large landmass, Sand Island.

Cameron and Rory were delighted to see colourful fish in the aquamarine water. There was so much life. Rainbow coloured creatures swam in the distance and a school of blue fish appeared just underneath the water's skin. Rory grinned and enjoyed the sun on his face. He seemed completely recovered from his earlier ordeal. The boys had never been on a speedboat before and were hyper with the new experience. They continued to be thronged by an impressive array of birds. These whirled through the air and landed on the boat. The boys watched as they landed and nestled on the beaches of Spit and East Island.

"I think they should rename that one Bird Island," Rory commented.

During the journey, the Harcourt family learnt all about Midway Atoll. "The islands are twenty-eight million years old," said Stephen, proudly. "It's a massive sanctuary for seabirds. We have millions of them. Really, millions. Not thousands."

"Yes, we figured," said Cameron.

Rory added, "It looks like most of the birds in the world are

151

right here."

"And the barrier reef is great for snorkelling and diving. The lagoon is about six miles across, and it's quite shallow. Look, you can see the edge of it way over there. And there. It's thick coral. By the way, you must see sunset at The Rusty Bucket. It's awesome. Dad can we take them?"

"The Rusty Bucket is one of the places on the island," Judah explained. "It's on the north-western tip. Yes, perhaps we can go there. It really is phenomenal when the sun goes down. The Creator is a genius."

"So, you know the Creator?" Daniel asked. "Back home it's a rare thing."

"We all know the Creator and the Rescuer here," laughed Judah. Then he went off on a tangent. "This place used to be an American naval installation, you know. But these days, it's just us. No uniformed soldiers. They all left a few decades ago. We don't have any tourists coming either. But we know what's going on in the world."

"There are forty-seven of us in total. Eight families and a few individuals, though we consider ourselves one big family really. And yes, we know the Rescuer. His Dunamis is with us." Judah's eyes glinted.

"Amazing," marvelled Arabella. It was the first thing she had said for a long while. She was enjoying having her husband back with her and knowing they were all safe at last.

It was afternoon on Sand Island. The weather was idyllic: warm and enjoyable. Judah steered them expertly to the top of the island. They came to one of two piers: long solid concrete structures edged with rectangular wooden beams and round poles. They both protruded from the sandy beach.

A welcoming party of young and old men, women and children, stood on the beach between the piers. The whole community was out: peering curiously, jabbering and nudging each other. It was the biggest crowd the Harcourts had seen for a while.

"They are eager to meet you," said Hannah graciously. "And

they would just love to feed you up."

Daniel and Arabella just smiled and smiled.

"You know what?" said Arabella. "I feel as though we have been running for such a long time, trying to escape one danger or another. To be surrounded by friendly people, it's almost more than I could dream of."

"That's wonderful to hear," said Hannah, climbing out of the boat and onto the pier. "Take my hand and mind your step. We'll have a drink in your hand in no time."

Chapter 20

Moments later, they were on the beach, overwhelmed with new names and faces. They were a colourful people from a range of nations. Daniel and Arabella spotted pale European faces, light and dark brown faces, and people with Far Eastern complexions. Arabella found it remarkable that so many different races could coexist in such a small place. The children were beautiful: sun-kissed, healthy and glowing. They instantly took to the Harcourt kids, finding them to be kindred spirits.

They were led to the centre of the broad beach, which was close by. There was a thick section of trees up the hill behind them, and two fat grey silos, presumably containing water or fuel. Daniel saw a few bicycles, a couple of Kawasaki golf carts and a jeep by the trees. That was how the people must get around, he figured.

Daniel asked about it. A friendly, unshaven man around a similar age to him answered in a soft accent from the American South. He had a patient demeanour and rectangular glasses.

"Hey, call me Doug. We walk a lot of the time. But when we want to transport things, we use the vehicles. The island is only a couple of miles square, so it's possible to walk wherever you want in very little time."

"How do you get your food?"

Judah, who was listening, answered, "We do grow some things here, and we even have a little mall. Though to be honest it's mainly used for the kids to play in now. We don't get any tourists anymore."

Doug picked up the thread. "We're pretty isolated here. We get most of our provisions from the other big islands. The Hawaiian Islands. Or from the States. The things we need come in by plane."

"Yes, we saw the airstrips on the other island."

"The main airstrip is on this one, Sand Island."

Their hosts encouraged them to sit down in comfortable beach chairs and relax by the sea. Daniel sat with Arabella by his side and the children at their feet in the sand. But Rory and Cameron just couldn't sit still. Before long, they were jumping and splashing in the shallows with the other children. It was wonderful for the parents to see them relaxing, knowing they were safe.

Next, the hosts passed around tall glasses of fresh fruit juices. The kids ran back. Daniel, Arabella and the children were offered a choice of coconut, passion fruit, pineapple, mango, banana or various berries. Rory chose mango and Cameron a mixture of juices. Then Rory wanted a mixture because his brother had been allowed one. So he got what he wanted too. But only after he'd finished his first glass, Arabella insisted.

A huge fire pit lay at the centre, ready for lighting later on when the sun went down. It was made from coal and dry wood and sat nestled on a low wooden frame in the sand. Judah, Hannah and Doug sat near Daniel and Arabella.

"This place is special isn't it," Arabella noted.

Judah smiled and said, "It has become a thin place over the years."

"A thin place?

"It's a place where heaven meets Earth. A place where it's easy to connect with the Creator through his Dunamis."

Daniel wondered whether Griffton was the opposite to a thin place. It was currently a place where darkness overshadowed the Earth. Daniel and Arabella were filled to overflowing with questions. However, the locals started to bring trays of seafood and rice down to the beach so the questions had to wait.

They set the food up on wide trays. The aromas immediately stirred up the appetites of the Harcourt family. They realised they hadn't eaten properly for a very long time.

They dined on coconut shrimp, fresh lobster and poached white fish. Dishes of fresh vegetables and rice accompanied the seafood. All the while, the locals chatted with their new friends, informing them of interesting facts about the island and their lives and learning whatever they could about the state of the world.

Many were not surprised at all by what was happening in Griffton and other parts of the United Kingdom. It fitted with what they knew about other countries. The enemy was tightening its iron grip on the globe. Places of refuge like Midway were rare in this age.

Night time fell. Somebody lit the fire pit. Hungry yellow tongues of fire licked the large circular bowl. Meanwhile, the sleepy orange sun breathed flames across the streaky clouds. The tops of the gentle waves responded by yielding burnt umber tones. The sea grew darker before them and their faces were lit by the flames.

"Can you take me to the Protector? Do you know where it is?" Daniel asked Judah.

"Yes. We will go tomorrow morning when it is safe. That is the appointed time."

"Safe?"

"A storm is coming tonight. It will pass. But it will hit where we need to go. In the morning it will be calm again."

"I see."

"Tonight you must rest. But first we will seek the Dunamis together."

"Yes, that would be a good idea. Do you know how to activate the Sea Protector?"

"No we don't. But the Dunamis tells us we will know when we get there. We believe one of you will know for certain."

"I hope so."

The forty-seven inhabitants of Midway Island, together with their four special guests, called on the Dunamis. They spent a glorious hour in his presence and he touched everybody, from the youngest to the oldest. He also wove their hearts together, giving them a strong affection for each other. Daniel and Arabella were overjoyed to have found a place of refuge and a group who knew the Rescuer like they did. They could learn so much from these people.

They left their time of encounter feeling rested and strengthened.

Then the locals entertained them with juggling and fire breathing, comic sketches and acoustic music. The local children did a funny dance as an old man played a twelve string guitar and sang into the night. Daniel and Arabella leaned back in their chairs and laughed, holding hands. Arabella turned to make an observation to the kids. She saw they were both fast asleep on the sand, Cameron's arm around Rory.

She gently tapped Daniel on the side and he leant over to look at them. He cooed in response and took the opportunity to kiss Arabella on the cheek. She turned back to her husband, dazzling him with her smile.

°°°°°12345°°°°°

In his sleep, Daniel heard the storm: squally rainfall in the distance. Thunder rumbled above. The wind raged. But he was only awake briefly and slipped back into dreams of the mezzanine. The rest of the family slept soundly in the empty guesthouse where they were stationed. The children were sleeping on comfortable chairs in the front room. He and Arabella had a proper bed which felt luxurious.

In the morning, Hannah brought them fresh coffee and home-baked bread. There was fresh juice as well, much to the kids' delight. It was a fresh and majestic morning. They were further south along the beach from where they'd gathered the previous night.

While his family rested, Daniel took himself for a walk back up to the beach where they had landed. It had been invaded by seabirds. He walked down the longer of the two piers, enjoying the sensation of having water on both sides.

There were times in his life when he took himself off and Samyaza would hassle him unexpectedly. These days, since he made a decision to follow the Rescuer, he felt only peace.

When he returned, Judah and Hannah were talking to the family outside the house. They sat on wooden chairs, waiting for him. Judah turned and said, "It's time to go."

Daniel nodded. The time for adventure was upon them again.

Judah's speedboat took them north away from the island. They crossed the deepest and longest part of the lagoon. Underneath them, the sea bed fell away to great depths.

Stephen explained, "If you jump off the boat and dive down, you would go down and down. You might not even get to the bottom." This made Rory gasp out loud.

"Really?"

"It is very deep here. See how the water is dark blue. Almost black," Judah talked loudly over the noise of the motor.

On they travelled until the water grew shallower again. It was light blue and clear. Many more fish appeared: red, blue and yellow ones. Small striped orange ones and huge grey ones. A manta ray slid through the water with incredible grace.

"Do you have turtles?" asked Rory.

"How about terrapins?" Cameron enquired.

"Are there sharks down there?" Rory added, not waiting for an answer.

"We have everything," said Stephen. He sat back in the boat and folded his arms, smiling proudly.

They arrived at the barrier reef that surrounded the atoll and protected it from the crushing waves beyond its borders. Judah cut the engine.

The coral displayed a spectacular spectrum of colour from pinks and purples to oranges, yellows and blues. Green and pink at the surface, the coral looked furry in the morning sun. It was made up of convoluted fingers, brain-like spheres and thick bushes.

"You're not meant to walk on it," said Judah. "But this time, we believe it's different. It's the only way to activate the Sea Protector."

"Should we all get out?" asked Daniel. "Do you know what we do next?"

"I don't know what we do from here," said Judah. Hannah smiled sweetly by his side.

"I don't know what to do either," said Stephen resignedly.

"I do," Rory piped up. "I need to get out. Let me get out," he sang excitedly.

"No, little one," warned Daniel. "This isn't the time to mess about. If we walk on that coral we could break it. And it's a whole ecosystem. It's all alive, and it keeps the fish alive."

"Just me. I'm light. Let me climb out. I think I know what to do. He told me. The Dunamis told me just now."

"I think he knows what he's doing, darling," said Arabella, touching Daniel's arm. "What did he say, sweetie?"

Rory scratched his head and said, "He said: the least of the least will dance before the King. I think that's me he's talking about."

"Did he say anything else? she asked.

Rory screwed up his face. "Oh yeah, I've got the words. He said: the least of the least will dance before the King on the water, pure and free."

Daniel laughed. "Well, Rory my boy. It sounds like this is your moment to save the world. The enemy tried to take you out. But he couldn't do it. You were born for such a time as this!"

Rory beamed, excited about dancing on the reef.

They helped him out and watched him step down from the boat until he was standing on the solid coral. The gentle waves lapped at his bare feet. He stood on a thick band of solid ground but the others were very conscious that beyond the reef, the dark waters dropped down to hundreds of feet.

"Be careful," called Arabella. She watched her little six-year-old boy anxiously.

"Should we all call on the Dunamis to help?" Cameron suggested. His father nodded in assent. So, they kept their eyes on Rory and quietly called on the Dunamis for his assistance. Rory started to dance a lovely, innocent dance.

"This is for the Creator, his Rescuer and their Dunamis," said Rory. "It's a 'you are amazing' dance; a 'thank you for your love' dance; and a 'please will you help protect us from the baddies' dance."

As he smiled, twirled and danced in innocence, faith, purity and worship, the reef began to shake. Behind him, a mountain rose up out of the water beyond. It was a wall of white that ascended into the air: an iceberg made of shiny cloud.

They could only glimpse it, so massive did it become. But they all realised what it was as soon as they caught the edge of the two massive wings.

The enormous Warrior Angel rose into the air and stood tall. Daniel felt the mysteries of the world were unfolding before him. He felt as though he were standing right up close to a mountain, looking up at the summit.

Before them was a white shimmering film: an immense curtain of light that brushed the sky. A sound emanated from it: a long chiming tune that changed every so often. It floated down on the breeze and spanned the ocean. The angel was singing to the Creator. He had started to fight on their behalf. They had activated their Sea Protector. Somehow, though they failed to grasp it fully, they sensed the battle had finally begun to turn in their favour.

Chapter 21

A wall of dry heat wafted up from the volcano crater ahead of them. Caleb, Serena and Micah gazed in wonder at the expansive caldera. It was enormous. The stone head watched silently by their side on the crater rim. There were no other people around.

"I think I know where we are," said Caleb. "We are in Tanzania. I've been here before. It's unmistakable. It's the Ngorongoro Crater."

"That's a word?" asked Micah.

Caleb looked at him and smirked. "You've got everything down there: hippos, cheetahs, zebra and wildebeest."

"It's breathtaking." Micah's eyes ran down the high sloping walls of the crater. They were predominantly brown but covered in dark grey cloud shadow. A green ridge spanned the horizon beneath a mid-blue sky. Bloated grey clouds hung in the air, shielding the forest-green basin from the scorching sun.

"There's a lake over there, which happens to be a soda lake: highly alkaline. Over there is a swamp. And the hippos like to gather in the springs over there," Caleb pointed out the various sites.

"Where on the Earth are we?"

"We're in East Africa. The west side of the Great Rift Valley. Have you heard of that? Good. Well that's where we are. This place was caused by a large volcano exploding and collapsing two or three million years ago. That's what they reckon. It's part of a series of old volcanoes."

"How do you know so much?"

"I travel a lot. I read lots of guidebooks. I also did long-haul and often went to Dar es Salaam. On one trip I did the hop over here to check out the crater. I've even done a safari down in the basin and stayed at that lodge over there," Caleb commented. He pointed to the far side of the rim. Serena and Micah followed his finger.

"Guess what it's called," he quizzed Serena.

"Tell me."

"It's called the Ngorongoro Serena Safari Lodge."

"You're making it up."

"They'll cook you up a zebra steak if you want."

"No thank you."

"Do you see all those black flecks on the green part over there? Those are most likely elephants standing on the grasslands. Or they could be buffalo. I'm not sure."

"You are right. They are elephants. But we don't have many at the moment," said a voice from behind them.

A small boy had crept up to them. He had curly black hair and a neat round nose. He wore a Manchester United T-shirt and shorts, with yellow plastic shoes on his feet that had holes on the top arranged in a pattern. His dark brown skin was visible through the holes.

"I knew that you would come. I am Andwele Juma. You can call me Ndege. I will take you where you need to go."

"To the Protector?" nodded Caleb.

"Yes." Ndege had a quick attention span, and cocked his head like a bird, eyeing each of them in turn.

"What happened to your hand there?" Caleb asked. "I see you are missing a finger. I hope you don't think me rude."

"It is okay. It was a month ago. It hurts me a lot. A devil took my finger. He was from the darkness. The Dunamis tells me the darkness has come. I am to help you push it back. You will help many people come out of the darkness and into the light."

"That's right. That's right," said Caleb thoughtfully. "Do you hear the Dunamis?"

"I know the Dunamis. And the Rescuer visits me sometimes. In my dreams he comes. He tells me stories. They told me about you."

Serena regarded the boy. She felt compassion for him and for the pain in his hand. Then she had a word of knowledge from the Dunamis. "I'm Serena. The Rescuer wants to heal your middle finger now," she said. "Will you give me your hand?"

"Give it to you?" His eyes widened.

"I mean place it in my hand," she smiled kindly, and he saw her eyes twinkle.

"Yes, I will do that."

Serena closed her eyes and asked the Rescuer to take away the boy's pain. Ndege visibly relaxed as the pain drained away from his middle finger. The shooting pains that had troubled him for the preceding weeks, and in fact all discomfort, left him.

Serena continued, "If I may be so bold, mighty Rescuer. I ask you for a creative miracle. Will you give this boy's finger back? To show your love, to show your glory?"

Ndege started to cry as a new finger grew from the stump of the previous one. Caleb, Micah and Serena felt as though they were watching a time-lapse video. Micah burst spontaneously into tears, moved by the miracle. Before their very eyes, a long brown middle finger poked out between the two shorter ones.

"Thank you, thank you," he blubbered, wriggling his fingers joyfully.

"Don't thank me. You know who to thank," Serena said quietly.

"So, how do we get to the Protector?"

"Do you know how to drive a jeep?" asked Ndege.

"Do I know how to drive a jeep?" Caleb grinned.

°°°°°*12345*°°°°°

Ndege lived close by with his family: his parents and his two sisters. They were away today in Arusha, buying furniture and food. It was four hours away by car. They were not expected back until nightfall.

They walked to the house which was twenty minutes away. As they went, Ndege explained that his family did not know the Rescuer yet. Even though he had told them many times about him and his power.

"They ignore me because I am small," he shrugged.

The house was a simple and pleasant affair. It was made of orange bricks and wooden beams, with a flat roof and two chimneys. He left them outside on the wooden porch with their packs. Meanwhile, he fetched the keys to the jeep which was parked outside.

The car was a closed-sided, pop top: a four-wheel affair. Bottle green. A layer of brown dirt across the bottom half. Two thick black tyres attached to the back. In effect, it was a small armoured tank, protecting the passengers from any unpredictable animals they might meet.

"It is easy to drive," said Ndege as he chucked the keys to Caleb.

"So why don't you drive it?"

"Are you kidding me? My father would kill me. Or anyone else driving his jeep."

"I see," mused Caleb. He noted that the vehicle had a local tour guide's permit on it.

"Is your father a guide by any chance?"

"Among other things, he does tours of the crater basin, yes."

"Okay then. Let's go."

The vehicle started up with a diesel cough and sputtered into life. Caleb soon got the hang of the controls. In seconds, he was driving the gang down the road. He enjoyed using the manual stick shift and transitioned between gears like a pro. Minutes later they approached the road that connected with the crater perimeter.

Caleb steered Ndege's father's jeep over the rim of the crater and onto a red, winding road that led to the bottom. He changed down in gear so he could approach the slope correctly. The sturdy jeep bounced and rocked, kicking up dust around its wheels. Serena and Micah held on in order to stay upright in their seats.

As they rounded each corner they caught appetising glimpses of the grassy savannah. The sunlight shone across a wide body of water in the distance. It transformed it into a dazzling pane of glass. Bright pink flamingos shone like lights at the water's edge.

"That is Lake Magadi, a shallow soda lake," Ndege informed them. Caleb nodded to Micah. "And on that side of it you can see forest. The Lerai Forest it is called."

Hardy green bushes squatted by the side of the road. These were interspersed with interesting flora and fauna that hid in the rocks.

The path grew browner and wound around and down at a shallow angle. It was a ten-minute journey that transported them to the short-grass plains at the bottom. Down here were numerous yellow fever trees: tall, dark-green acacias that stood their ground resolutely in the dry land.

Before long, they were spotting celebrated African mammals: Thompson's and Grant's gazelles and black rhino, which wandered happily in the open grasslands. They cheerily pointed them out to each other, delighted to have spotted so much game.

"Astounding. How have I never come here before?" Serena said.

"Where is it we have to go?" asked Caleb. "Do you know, Ndege? Or you, Serena?" Serena shook her head.

"The Dunamis says we must go to the centre of the basin. You will know what to do then. That is all he has given me. Follow the path this way. You will come to a crossroads. Take the right and head for the lake. Then we will park and get out."

"Is it safe?"

"There is a rifle under the back seat," Ndege replied.

Down on the crater floor, by the lake, the grass was dark orange in the sunlight. The majestic sides of the crater rose up around them. They formed a circle of undulating ridges. They looked hazy because they were so far away. But it was possible to pick out the vertical lines that resembled the bottom part of a velvet dress flowing down to the ground.

Lake Magadi was the dominant feature of the Ngorongoro crater floor. The large pool of dark blue water was covered in flamingos. They thronged the sides and sat like pink lily pads on the surface of the lake. On the other side was a herd of ten stripy zebra, tossing their heads in the air. Further along were twenty or thirty angular brown wildebeest. They lazily chewed the short yellowing grass.

Caleb enjoyed the jabbering of the birds and the neighing of the zebra. An almost imperceptible breeze played about their faces as they gathered by the jeep. The last bit of the ride had been bumpy so it was nice to get out.

Micah ran his fingers through his long hair and watched the flamingos. He wandered down near the water's edge to get a better view. It looked safe enough. The others stood near the car, enjoying the sunshine and the beauty of the crater.

"So, what now?" Micah called back. He watched the graceful forms of the zebra as they snacked on the tall grass and swished their tails.

"We stay very still," said Ndege in a quiet, theatrical hiss.

"Why?" Micah turned around.

"Lions," breathed Ndege, indicating their location with a nod. "We need to get back in the jeep quickly."

A male lion with a huge, furry mane and sleepy eyes looked at them across the distance. His body was thin and hungry looking. He was lying by a lone tree that afforded him a minimal amount of shade. Its long branches stretched outwards to catch as many rays as they could.

The lion wrinkled his soft black nose which lay at the centre of a serious-looking face. At the top of his tufty head was a patch of black hair, surrounded by straw-coloured strands.

Nearby was another lion: a female. She looked over calmly. The way her features were arranged made her appear to smile at them. She was sleek and lean with pointed ears and winking eyes.

Three smaller cubs lay by her feet, cute baby cats with tight sandy fur. They appeared to be asleep, though every so often, one of them would twitch a paw, a leg or a tail.

"No sudden movements," said Ndege. "That is the general rule."

The big lion started to walk towards them at a leisurely pace. He scowled, licking his broad black lips and showing his teeth. They looked like a row of pale white knives.

"I left the rifle in the jeep. I'm going to open the front door. Follow me inside."

"Wait for me!" Micah called from the water's edge. He started to move quickly towards the others. They were at least thirty paces away. Serena climbed into the jeep behind Ndege.

"Don't run," hissed Caleb. The lion quickened his strides. He had chosen to ignore them and go for Micah instead.

"What do I do? Help!" yelped Micah. He froze.

Caleb stepped away from the vehicle. He called on the Dunamis. "Mighty Dunamis. Rescuer, my friend. Deliver us," he said with urgency.

The lion stopped in its tracks. He stood an equal distance between Micah and Caleb. Suddenly he turned his head towards Caleb and said, in a low growl, "It's time. Activate the Protector."

Caleb watched in amazement as the creature walked away to join his family, swinging his long tail behind him.

The word of the Rescuer came to Ndege while he was hiding in the jeep. He turned to tell Serena who was still reeling from witnessing the close shave outside. But she had left the jeep, springing out onto the grass to hug Caleb.

"Are you all right my darling?"

"I'm fine. And Micah's fine. Did you see that? I've seen the Dunamis do a lot of things in my time. He's certainly got me out of some scrapes. But that was right up there with the best of them."

Micah ran up to them with his mouth open.

"Did you see that? He spoke, didn't he? But I didn't hear him.

Did he say something to you? Why did he walk away?"

"I believe we were protected today. The Dunamis told me, through the lion, that now is the time."

"I heard him!" Ndege shouted. "I heard the voice of the Dunamis!"

"Yes, I know," said Caleb.

"No, he told me in the jeep what we must do." Ndege waved his little arms about, joggling his baseball cap.

"What did he say?" asked Serena.

"He said: the least of the least will dance before the King on the earth, pure and free."

"He's talking about you," said Arabella. She stroked his face which made him blush. "You said it yourself. Your family doesn't listen to you because you are small. It makes you the least of the least. But the King considers you to be worthy. You must activate the Land Protector."

"What, right here?"

"Why not!" said Caleb.

"Why don't you come over here to the lake?" suggested Micah. He took Ndege's arm and led him to a space by the water's edge. "We could both dance. It will be fun. I haven't danced for a long time!"

So, side by side, Micah the nineteen-year-old and Ndege who was several years his junior, started to hop and jump on the bank of the lake. They were two brothers united by the Dunamis. Serena clapped and Caleb whooped while they danced. They celebrated the King who held the world in his hands. They danced before the one who loved them and watched over them in both dark and joyful times. And then it happened.

The crater floor trembled. Up from the ground rose a wall of flickering light. A mound became a hill that became a mountain. It towered above them, rising slowly until it reached its full height. Filmy and translucent it glistened and shone.

Caleb gawped. It was magnificent. He craned his neck to view the skyscraper-high Warrior Angel. It was only possible to catch a glimpse: the curve of a wing feather. The hem of a robe.

A new song filled the air. The angel was singing and the music was a mighty and powerful clarion call. It was the sound of a thousand chimes ringing. The tune undulated, filling the air and then tailing off only to rise up again.

The Protector of the Land had gone into battle.

Chapter 22

The sea of boys surged towards Rachel, Eddie and Lake. The three of them sprang from mound to mound along the riverbank. They rushed along without looking back, keeping to the same order they had in the water. Eddie led the way, Rachel took the middle and Lake followed. Bouncing on her toes, Rachel kept up with Eddie. She wasn't concerned about Lake. He was fit and fast.

Lake turned round quickly to check how they were doing. "We're okay. Keep moving. They haven't managed to gain on us."

They leapt over a fallen tree that overhung the river. Eddie landed heavily, hurting his knee. It slowed him down a little, but Rachel encouraged him to keep going.

"We can't let them catch us," panicked Rachel.

The sound of tramping feet pursued them. The path by the river was beset by small mossy rocks and dry twigs. There were chunky purple bushes to the right of them.

Jogging now, Eddie, Rachel and Lake panted a little with the exertion. Theoretically, they shouldn't be growing tired in the mezzanine. Rachel thought it must be psychological.

The ground was clear up ahead of them. It became scrubland again, open on all sides except for the river. The ground became easier to run on as well. It was flatter and more uniform.

Intimidated by their pursuers, they picked up their pace again. Even Eddie managed to find an extra spurt to shift his big body faster across the ground.

And then a thought came to Rachel like a blow. "What are we doing?" she said under her breath. "What is there to be scared of? The Dunamis is with us."

She called to Eddie, "We need to stop. We need to face them. Trust me. We can do this."

"Are you sure?" Eddie knew that before long the army of Olms would be upon them. They actually had very little choice. It wasn't possible to outrun them. "Okay then," he conceded.

"Are you guys crazy? We can't just stop. They'll eat us alive."

"No. We have to stop," panted Rachel.

She stopped running. Lake went past her but Eddie halted immediately.

Holding her hand up to the boys, Rachel shouted, "Stop! In the name of the Rescuer I command you to stop."

Her direct order arrested their attack. The group of innumerable albino orphans stopped in their tracks. They reassembled as a single mob standing on the bank with their eyes fixed on her.

"Do you see my hair?" shouted Rachel like a lunatic. "It's white now! Do you know what that means? Do you?"

There was no response. However, they didn't move forward either.

"It means you can't touch me now, you creepy losers. I'm protected. All three of us. We are protected," Rachel was screaming now.

For the first time, the group of boys showed some emotion. They hissed and seethed. They'd lost their father, Zed the shape shifter, and were livid. They lusted for revenge.

"I think it's time to move on," Rachel said to Lake. Eddie nodded. He noticed the boys were starting to walk towards them.

"It doesn't look like they're giving up."

"Oh, for goodness sake," said Rachel, exasperated. She turned back towards the crowd. Just then, a group of Warrior Angels flew down and landed on the path between them. The imposing beings held their swords out towards the spawners. Meanwhile, one of the angels indicated to Rachel that she should keep going.

"Thank you," she mouthed in awe. Then she and the others escaped.

The boys fell upon the angels and tried to bite them. But they were no match for the mighty swords of the angel army. As metal flashed and found its mark, the spawners dropped like flies. Soon, the angels reduced them down from a hundred to a few dozen. They continued to chop and slash, knee deep in bodies.

Rachel ran away with sounds of battle fading into the background.

°°°°°*12345*°°°°°°

At long last they saw it. The stone head rose out of the river bank like a fat grey tree trunk. It waited for them, facing away from the water and looking over the dry valley. There were low mountains at the periphery made of striking black and red rock. A web of hanging rocks was suspended above the ground. It created a netting effect, scattering grey shadows across the valley.

A patchwork of mauve and cherry clouds meshed together in the sky above. They sent a sprinkling of rain over the land. Rachel felt the droplets on her head and hands.

"Man, that was too close for comfort. Let's get out of this crazy place," said Lake.

"Great idea," Eddie agreed.

"It reminds me of a joke," added Lake.

"Everything reminds you of a joke," groaned Rachel.

"So, this man says to the ticket agent: I want to buy a plane ticket for Norwald. For a holiday, you know? So the ticket agent searches his bookings and says: Norwald? Let me find that. Hmm... never heard of it. Let me see... Norwald. I don't see Norwald listed and I can't find it on the map. Just where is Norwald anyway? The man replies: Over there. He's my brother!"

"Lake, that is terrible," said Rachel, rolling her eyes. Eddie seemed to like it though, and chuckled to himself.

"Norwald," he said. "That's funny."

"If you like that one, I've got an even better one," Lake quipped.

Out of nowhere, a giant black demon swooped down from the clouds and stood between them and the stone head.

"Woah," Lake yelped. They froze. Three others landed beside them, forming a barrier. They fanned open their black wings. Petrified, Lake jumped back. He turned to run, his face pale and rigid. Eddie, too, began to bolt. Only Rachel remained calm. Encouraged by her earlier success with the spawners, she drove the fear from her mind.

Rachel closed her eyes and sat down on the ground.

"Rachel, run!" shouted Lake.

She held her hand up before her, eyes still closed. She began to laugh, against her nature and against all reason. It was the laughter of a little girl amused by a butterfly or some floating bubbles. It wasn't particularly loud, but it was innocent and peaceful. The demons stood and glowered at her. The distance between her and them was about a hundred metres. Perfectly calm now, Rachel lifted her head and opened her eyes to look at them.

Without any warning the creatures started to bear down on her. They ran and hopped like great crows shifting their bulk along the ground.

"You guys go," she heard herself saying. "Go! I'm staying here."

Her body buzzed with the presence of the Dunamis. She was at peace with the world. If her time had come to die, then she would die knowing the enemy hadn't got to her. She would pass from this world into the Rescuer's arms knowing that she had overcome the fear and dread in her life. She had been scared for far too long. It was pointless. It was draining. It held her back from being everything she was created to be.

She looked up again, feeling as though she were underwater, looking at a flock of birds hovering over the water's surface, distorted by the liquid skin. The four black bats continued to run at her. Their eyes were locked on her. Their talons and teeth ready to rip into her. But she was peaceful and prepared.

Rachel closed her eyes, trusting the Rescuer, her wonderful

King. She knew that whether she lived or died she would be with him. To live was a bonus but to die was better. She won both ways. He had rescued her and she loved him. He had filled her with hope and turned her hair white so she would never forget.

And she was weary. She had seen so much and travelled so far. Her life had been a battle. She was tired of fighting. It hadn't been a bad year. Yes, she had faced the Malkin and the demons and lost. But she had regained friendship with her father and forged a new relationship with the Rescuer. Once she stepped out of this life, she would be reunited with him and embrace her mother again. She would be in a place where there was no more suffering or death. No more troubles. Only rest.

Besides, Eddie and Lake could finish the race now. She would happily sacrifice herself for them. So they could escape. She sang quietly to herself, to her Rescuer King, the one who had filled her with fire and new life. Yes, the others could sprint for the stone head while the demons ripped her apart. Her death meant they would be able to find and activate their Protector and save the human race.

Rachel breathed out and waited. The sound of loud scuffling and guttural cries arrested her. Her eyes popped open. The four demons lay in heaps on the ground in front of her. At their backs was a troupe of Warrior Angels. They stood tall, their robes and faces radiant. Their long swords were covered in dark sticky blood. Rachel collapsed back onto the path and laughed with relief.

Eddie and Lake ran up to her, their minds reeling.

When the demons had struck, they were stunned, finding themselves incapable of deciding whether to stay or run. In that instant, both of them feared for Rachel's safety. Neither of them wanted to leave her alone, but still they were defenceless. They watched in terror as she sat down on the ground. The scene played out in both of their heads: Rachel being engulfed by a wave of dark, destructive evil. Powerless, they watched them rush at her. Equally helpless, they saw the winged liberators appear from the sky, land behind the attackers and swing their swords.

It was over in minutes.

With Eddie on one side and Lake on the other, they held onto Rachel. They helped her up to a sitting position.

"Thank you. Thank you so much," Eddie said. Lake jabbered incoherently, but managed to repeatedly thank the angels and apologise to Rachel for not being by her side. Rachel gazed up in wonder at the warriors, her champions.

One of them stepped forward and spoke in a voice that resembled harp music. "The way is clear now. Go. You have work to do. And do not be afraid."

The angels stood to one side as Eddie, Rachel and Lake walked slowly to the stone head. They passed the dead bodies of the monsters. As they walked by, the black leathery mounds threatened to spring to life and attack again. But they stayed inert, defeated. They posed no danger now. The rain fell once more from the portly cumulonimbus clouds above. It was light at first, but quickly grew more persistent. By the time they were standing in front of the portal, the rain was falling heavily. Eddie took the lead.

"Are you two ready?" he checked. His white hair was plastered to his forehead. He grinned incongruously.

Rachel turned to Lake: her hair wet and her dark eyes searching. He looked back at her and smiled. Impulsively, she grabbed his hand and held it tight. He was her handsome Lake and she loved him. He was her fellow adventurer in life. He maintained his sense of humour through everything, and he cared deeply about her. That was all she needed.

"Together?" she asked.

"Together," he said.

Eddie nodded to them, turned and disappeared through the doorway. Holding hands, Rachel and Lake followed. Once they were sure they had gone, the angels took off into the sky.

Chapter 23

Mount Jomolhari is part of the Himalaya range in western Bhutan. Eddie, Rachel and Lake emerged onto the slopes of this desolate mountain.

Overlooking the Chumbi Valley and residing in Jigme Dorji National Park, Jomolhari is the second highest peak in Bhutan. It straddles the border of Yadong County in Tibet and the Thimphu district of Bhutan. Its soaring north face rises eight thousand nine hundred feet above the barren plains; twenty-four thousand feet above sea level.

"This is ridiculous!" shouted Lake over the howling wind. Icy snow showers rained down on them as they scrambled to pull on their winter coats. Lake repeatedly tried to brush the powder off his body but he ended up covered all over again. He gave up on being snow-free and fastened up his coat in desperation.

Long hours of carrying it over his arm were finally paying off. Caleb had been right in suggesting they come properly equipped. So now, Lake was overjoyed to be wearing his thick cotton shirt and combat trousers. He would have preferred a T-shirt and shorts in the mezzanine but now it all made sense.

"What is this frozen wasteland?" asked Eddie exasperated. They blinked, and shaded their eyes against the brilliant whiteness that surrounded them. The cold air froze their noses and throats. Rachel put her backpack around her shoulders and hugged her body. They were high up on a mountainside overlooking an icy gorge. In front of them they could see an arc of glaciated mountain peaks. Their sharp points speared the sky. With wide eyes, Rachel traced the graceful lines rising and falling across the valley. She wondered at the immensity of it all.

"Welcome to Bhutan, I guess," said Rachel.

"What?" called Lake. It was difficult to hear each other over the noise of the wind.

The stone head stood behind them. It was completely covered in snow except for the place they had walked through. A tall ridge of snow sat on its head like a top hat.

Eddie spotted a sheltered area down a steep slope. He indicated it to them and started to lead. The path proved to be slippery but they made it down to a plateau by moving slowly and carefully. The rock formation at the bottom gave them some shelter from the snow. They huddled together for warmth.

"What you think we do?" asked Lake.

"I have no idea," said Rachel.

"It's the river all over again. We need to listen out for the Dunamis," said Eddie. "Especially you, Lake."

"Why me?"

"Because you heard him last time. Remember? He told you we should swim under the rock. That turned out to be the right thing to do."

"Oh yeah. I'll listen out." Lake brushed the snow out of his hair and put his hood up for extra warmth. He sniffed and looked up. The sky was a band of white. The snow relented a little. It drifted down in large flakes. Lake felt mild vertigo as he glanced down into the treacherous valley. There was a frozen lake at the base, reflecting the mountain. Tiers of ice and patches of shadow were displayed on its surface, culminating in a sharp but rounded point.

"If we stay here, we'll freeze to death," Rachel observed.

"So what do you think we should do? If we go up, it can only get colder."

"Let's stay close to the rocks here and go and explore," Eddie suggested. "Meanwhile, listen hard and see if the Dunamis tells you anything. Me, I've got nothing."

Cautiously they made their way around the rocky wall, still shielded slightly from the elements. Hard grey rock lay underfoot. A build-up of snow formed all around. The going was tough but they persevered. Rachel could no longer feel her fingers, despite wearing the gloves she'd brought from home.

Beyond the place where they had stopped, the ground widened and they felt more secure crossing it. In order to go over the edge and down into the valley they would have to run and slide. It widened further into a snowy plateau with small rocks peeking out.

In the midst of the white landscape they saw a bright blue canvas tent. It was nestled beside a steep snowy slope that stretched upwards towards the body of the mountain. The tent was rectangular with a sloping roof. Its white guy ropes were pulled taught and jammed into the ground at right angles. The shelter was zipped closed.

There were a couple of other signs of life apart from the tent itself. The snow around it had been trampled and there was some black plastic sticking out of a mound of snow close by the tent. It looked like a tool of some sort.

Eddie and Lake looked at each other. Together, they converged on the tent. They knew if they didn't do something, they would perish. Although they had warm coats, they lacked additional clothing: scarves and hats. This big blue tent was their only hope right now. It could mean shelter, food or friendship. They were happy to take anything right now.

"Hey," shouted Eddie as he skidded across the ground towards the tent. "Anybody home?" Lake was by his side.

Nobody answered so he decided to try unzipping the tent. The zipping mechanism had thick metal teeth and the fabric was hard wearing. As he started to pull the metal fastening up with his numb fingers, Eddie and Lake heard muffled screams from behind them. They turned back to check on Rachel.

They glimpsed two tall men in leather jackets, one on either side of Rachel. One put his hand over her mouth. They snatched her quickly and expertly and quickly dragged her off. She was thrown over a shoulder, kicking and screaming. In seconds the men vanished around the corner.

Eddie and Lake bolted after them. Lake skidded. Eddie carried on going. He got as far as the place they had taken her. Then he saw them quickly descend the slopes in the distance. Lake was a few feet behind him.

Eddie decided to give chase, determined to save his daughter. "Rachel!" he shouted. His voice was raw with the cold.

He set off after them, skidding and slipping down the snowy slope. They were much faster, better prepared for this climate. He frequently had to put his hands out to steady himself. Soon, he realised it was impossible to keep up with them. He saw them in the distance, further down the mountainside. Lake caught up with him, being younger and fitter.

"They're getting away with her," panted Eddie.

"I won't let that happen," said Lake, resolutely.

"Go on then. You go. Stop them!"

Lake passed Eddie and tripped and skipped down the slopes. He lost sight of the men but kept going. The ground was hazardous. It was difficult to slow down but he did his best. He had to employ all of his skating skills of balance, agility, poise and the ability to come to a halt quickly. He saw the three of them even further down. Two men in brown and black and Rachel being hauled like a sack of potatoes. She was no longer struggling. She just lay on the man's shoulder, limp. He wondered if they had knocked her out.

There was a cry from behind him. It was the deep throated roar of a man.

"Eddie?" Lake yelled back up the mountain. But there was no more noise. Just the whistling of the wind and the soft sound of snow falling.

"What do I do? What do I do?" Lake asked himself. He couldn't leave Rachel. He needed to know if Eddie was all right. He loved Rachel. But if he left Eddie and he was injured, that would be a bad choice too.

He made a snap decision. He would check on Eddie first. Then together they would go down and try to find Rachel.

Hurriedly, Lake doubled back. He dragged himself back up the path, calling out for Eddie every so often.

He found him sitting on the hard ground with his head down.

"Are you all right?"

"I twisted my ankle," said Eddie, mournfully. Then he added, "They took her. They took my little girl." He shook his head. "What are we to do?"

"I don't know," said Lake. "I guess we should call on the Dunamis. Isn't that the right thing to do?"

"I don't know," said Eddie. "I don't know. They took her and she's gone. I couldn't protect her."

"She's a tough girl," said Lake. "You saw what she did back there with those horrible monsters? She stayed calm and we were okay. Anyway, we're not going to give up. Right? We'll go down together. We'll find her."

°°°°°12345°°°°°

Eddie leaned heavily on Lake as he hobbled down the mountain slope. Although Lake was strong, he still found Eddie's bulky frame a challenge. Particularly on these icy paths. There wasn't an official route because the mountain was so rarely visited. The only tracks up and down the mountain were ones you created yourself. Consequently, it was hard going for both Eddie and Lake.

Eddie winced every so often as he put his full weight on his ankle. Being a large man, this caused him considerable discomfort. He apologised continually but Lake batted it back.

They were both subdued. Lost in thought. Losing Rachel was a major blow: inconceivable in fact. They were both wearied by the

180

freezing conditions. Their noses were running. Their faces were numb. The feeling had left their fingers. Eddie's torso ached with the frigid air that invaded his lungs. Besides this, their eyes were painful, dazzled by the bright white that was all around them and stretched from the sky to the ground.

The mountainside was endless. There was nowhere to stop so they had to keep moving. It took a very long time to get down. At long last they came to a flatter area. They still couldn't see any sign of the men. The snow flurries that came down would surely hide any tracks they made – if any tracks were to be found.

"This is desperate," puffed Eddie. "Are you hearing anything from the Dunamis?"

"Nothing. You?"

"Nope."

"So how does it work? Is he having a laugh? The Rescuer, I mean." Lake queried.

"No, he's not having a laugh. Have you met him?"

"No."

"There are forces ranged against us, Lake. Like I said in the mezzanine, he could step in and fix it all. But it's a complex system in motion. There are lots of things we don't understand. There's a bigger picture than the one we can see. A much bigger picture. But you need to know that he is good and he does care. And he isn't having a laugh. I know. I've met him. And to know him is to trust him. Even when things look dark."

"I'll take your word for it," smirked Lake.

They spotted a flat-roofed building down below: a wooden lodge. There were snow-covered trees nearby. White hills sloped away at forty-five degrees, with a couple of sharp black rocks sticking out halfway up.

"Over there," said Lake.

"Yeah, let's check it out."

"Carefully though."

"I can't see anyone around."

"Maybe they've taken her inside," said Lake.

Together they walked down to the structure. It had a simple wooden door in the middle of it and its roof was covered by a thick wedge of snow. A chimney poked through the roof, with a pointed snow protector at the top. There were two windows in the front. Tall piles of compacted snow sat on either side of the door. There was no sound within and no vehicle tracks or signs of activity. Lake looked through one of the windowpanes. It was dark inside.

"Eddie, you stay here. Keep watch. I'll check the back. Then we'll try the door."

Eddie nodded in assent and leaned heavily on the side of the house.

Lake stomped around the back. The building backed onto a slope but there was sufficient space to walk around the perimeter. He quickly circled the house while Eddie turned and checked the surroundings. There were no windows at the back, just the vertical planks of wood that formed the walls. Eddie was relieved to see Lake re-emerge. They nodded to each other.

"She must be in here," said Lake. "I can't see anywhere else they might have taken her. There's only so far you can carry someone. Unless they have a helicopter or something, they must still be here. I'm going to try the door."

"Okay. But steady. They might be armed," Eddie warned.

Lake put his hand on the door handle. Flooded with adrenalin, he pushed down hard and pressed his weight against the door. It swung open quickly. Capitalising on the momentum, Lake rushed into the building with his fists up. He cast his gaze around, expecting to find a room full of gangsters or snow leopards.

The house was empty. There was a single room, generous in size. It was lit from the outside by the white sky and the gleaming snow. The milky light gave everything an ethereal glow. Although it was furnished, there was very little in the way of creature comforts. Lake saw a simple bed covered by a cream blanket; a couple of functional chairs; a sink; a fireplace and a few other things. But Rachel wasn't there and neither were the men. No one was home.

"Eddie," he shouted out. "She's not in here. Come in. It's a bit warmer inside. There's a chair you can sit on. Rest your ankle before we move on."

There was no reply from Eddie. He tried calling out again. All that returned to him was the cold silence of the mountains.

Chapter 24

The Watchers and the Nephilim exploded into Western Europe. Their trail of destruction stretched from the mountains of Nepal through Kyrgyzstan and Azerbaijan to Turkey and Bulgaria. The travellers gathered pace as they went. Samyaza had his end goal in mind and drove the others on. No respecter of human life, the eternal beings brought a carnival of disaster with them. They mangled roads and bridges wherever they went, bringing down tall and short buildings alike.

They set upon the towns and cities like locusts descending. Mixed with the screams of the people were their deafening roars.

As they progressed, Samyaza sent individual members of his Grigori and Nephilim family off to key locations to take up residence. He was building a cast-iron network of crazed power-mongers, unpredictable and brutal in their desire to control.

As they raged, they preyed upon whoever they chose: businessmen, vagrants, shop assistants, farmers or politicians. Everyone was the same under their hateful gaze. Created beings were their enemy and it was time to punish them, extract their worship by force, or destroy them completely.

°°°°°12345°°°°°

As Eddie waited for Lake, he became engulfed in a noxious cloud of stench. Looking up, Eddie realised that a hooded man was standing before him. Aghast, he wondered where he'd come from. He certainly wasn't there a minute ago.

The dark figure thrust a sharp blade towards him. Gasping, Eddie looked down and watched helplessly as it sank into his chest. The pain lasted an instant, and strangely, no lingering sting remained.

Eddie looked up and saw the Rescuer, watching him from the centre of the snowy plateau, beyond his cowardly attacker. The broad-shouldered man sat tall on his white stallion and locked eyes with him. Nodding once, he said, simply, "It's time to go home."

Eddie started to laugh.

°°°°°*12345*°°°°°

Snowflakes began to fall on Eddie's lifeless body. Vibrant blood seeped into the snow beneath him. It flowed from the wound in his chest. Horrified, Lake stared at him. He crouched down to touch Eddie's exposed hand. Instinctively, he tried to stop the flow of blood. But it was like putting his hand on a beefsteak that lay on a chopping board. It was too late to help.

The surreal moment swallowed him whole. It was hard to make sense of what he witnessed. It was definitely Eddie with his white hair, sturdy body and big hands. His eyes were closed and there was a smile on his face. He looked peaceful; joyful even, thought Lake. It made him marvel: why was the big man so composed?

He dragged his eyes away from Eddie's form in order to calculate the degree of danger he was in. Lake stood up slowly. His eyes flicked across the white ground. He checked the mountain slopes, glancing from tree to tree and mound to mound. There was nothing out there. The enemy was hiding, invisible or gone.

He looked back to the house. But like Eddie, it was motionless. It suddenly struck him. Rachel was taken. Eddie was dead. He was alone in Bhutan. His parents were back in Griffton. Caleb, Daniel and the others were miles away. They weren't even in the same country. Alone. He was alone. The feeling resonated and grew, expanding into full-blown panic.

His mind was clouded but he needed to act. He decided to try to get Eddie inside the house. It felt like the right thing to do. He tried pulling his arms but couldn't shift him. He even grabbed his middle. He was too heavy. Lake ended up covered in Eddie's blood. It was a pointless exercise and only served to heighten his panic. He would have to leave the body out there in this outdoor freezer. It was starting to get even colder and the sky wasn't as bright as earlier. Snow was beginning to fall once more. A nasty Arctic gale also entered the plateau.

Lake sat on the ground next to Eddie. He found himself overwhelmed by a wave of emotion. Desperate and empty, he threw his head back and roared. After that, he found it difficult to limit the number of tears that he cried. He wept freely and unreservedly. Alone. He was alone. Sobs overtook his body, making him shake with grief and coldness. The snowfall grew more intense.

Another emotion washed over him. Fear. Not only was he alone, he was also being hunted. A shadowy figure materialised at the edge of his vision. He wasn't alone. Evil had followed him from the mezzanine. He stood up. He had a strong desire to flee the killer. Quickly. Feeling that his attacker was to the right of him, he bolted for the trees to the left. He pounded the snow with his feet but made it to the tree line alive. Safe for now.

Panting, he looked out to see where the figure had gone. While he stooped to peek out from behind the tree trunk, the fear came again. The shadowy creature was to the left of him. It was by his side. He was sure of it. Tormented, he ran into the open, looking back. It wasn't there. He shot glances all around him.

"Where are you?" He jabbered, spinning in a circle. He was convinced it was at his back. It was behind him, he was sure. But was it? He ran again, sliding across the icy snow. The broad path led down a slope and he quickly gained access to it. He figured it must be the way the men escaped. Down and out.

But as it opened up, all he could see was more of the same: snowy plains and glacial sheets that rolled for miles. At their edges were rocky ascents and steep drops. There was nowhere to go.

He finally shook the feeling of being pursued though. By now, a snowstorm had blown up. Tiny white flecks filled his vision. The temperature started to plummet. Lake wedged his fingers into his coat pockets but the feeling didn't return to them.

He trudged back up the hill to the enclosure where the building stood. It was still devoid of people or vehicles. There were no clues as to who or what had killed Eddie. It could have been a knife or a bullet.

He walked over to the house, treading through thick snow. Eddie was completely covered by a layer of the white stuff. He crouched down and brushed it off with his arm, but knew it would just build up again. It was only a matter of time.

Should he go back to the stone head? The path was steep and he might not even find the way back. They had zigzagged a couple of times on the way down but he might remember the route. It was worth a try.

It meant he could go back into the mezzanine and get some help. The angels would come to his aid, surely? He made a snap decision to climb back up the mountain.

He found the place where they had entered this part of the range. It was difficult to see through the blizzard but he tried. Though his legs were frozen and tired, he picked his way back up the mountain slopes.

It took a painfully long time, during which the blizzard relented. A cold wind was all that was left as a gift for Lake. By the time he reached the summit and found the stone head, night-time was approaching, though only a light snow fell. The majestic structure stood in front of him, a broad column of snow-covered stone. White lines marked out its features. It looked like an old-man version of the stone head on Griffton Cliff.

Lake put his hand on the face. He felt the hard surface pushing back against his wrist. Nothing happened. It remained a solid stone monument. The doorway was not open to him.

"Oh, come on!" He cried out, leaning his shoulder against it. The wind started to pick up. "Open up!" He commanded. Nothing happened. He waited, shouted and even called on the Dunamis. It was useless. The portal was shut. It didn't even feel like giving him an electric shock.

He was out of options. The only way for him to survive was to go back down to the house. To make matters worse, the blizzard was back and darkness was coming.

Lake turned, set his mind on survival and walked carefully back to the top of the slope. His body ached. His legs were made of concrete. There was no choice though, he had to make the treacherous descent.

It was a gruelling walk, impacting his knees and ankles. Sometimes he slipped and slid; sometimes he caught his foot on a rock. He fell twice. But somehow he made it back to the house. It was very difficult to see now and his emotions were starting to shut down. He had to leave Eddie outside, a pile of snow acting as his burial mound.

It rested heavily on him. He'd let Eddie down. He had completely failed to rescue Rachel. There was no way he could activate the Air Protector without them. He didn't even know what it was, let alone where to go. His worst nightmares had become reality. He was at the end of himself.

With hooded eyes and a heavy heart, Lake pushed open the door of the house and went inside. He locked it from the inside and turned to have a proper look at the lodge. It looked like a place of refuge, somewhere that climbers used on their way up. There were no ornaments or signs of ownership.

Survival on his mind, he found food in the cupboards: canned beans, packets of dry foodstuff, powdered milk and even a few cans of soft drinks. He drank a sugary liquid from an unfamiliar brand and snacked on some dry crackers. Then he turned his attention to the fire. It had grown bitterly cold. Freezing air came down from the chimney stack. There was a basket of wood nearby, with paper and matches to start a fire. The logs were roughly hewn but they were perfect.

After a few attempts, Lake built a crackling fire. He looked at it blankly and took off his coat and shoes. Although his skin was starting to thaw, his emotions weren't. The fire started to heat the small one-room bungalow. There was a toilet in the corner, and he took advantage of this. Then Lake climbed into the bed, pulled the blanket over him and lay down to rest. He felt hollow, lonely and desperate.

Lake found himself crying wearily as he fell asleep, begging the Creator to take pity on him. Calling on the Rescuer and his Dunamis to help. Meanwhile, the fire crackled, lapping at the logs and consuming them. The gift of sleep soon came to Lake and he collapsed into its embrace.

°°°°°12345°°°°°

José Antonio Diez was getting sick of the Dream Fighters pushing him around. He knew he was powerless to do anything about it, though, which just made it worse. They were bullies and cowards as far as he was concerned. They were not the heroes he thought they were. As time passed, he wondered whether the three men were right. The men they helped throw into the stone head.

On the walk down to the head, the men had tried to warn them the Dream Fighters might not be what they seemed. At the time, he thought they were trying to trick him and his brother Diego. He knew they wanted to escape so they would say anything.

What was it the thin old man had said? "Just because they rescued you from your enemies, doesn't mean that they are not the enemy themselves." It was definitely a warning. And he should have paid attention.

The most troublesome one was Pulto, the boss guy. He was a big, bad warrior who was rarely without his leather armour and red and black sash. He pushed the boys around and was nasty to the girls. Plus he was lazy, always sitting in Papa's chair while everyone else did the work. He even had Papa running around fetching and carrying for him. To start with, the boys found it amusing. But they soon recognised that these men did not respect their father one bit.

To start with it was fun for them, being trained as fighters. They got to wear armour and practice sword drills. It was great fun stabbing scarecrows and sparring with each other. But this didn't last very long. They still had to farm the soybean crops and work as hard as they ever had. Even harder perhaps. So life was very much as it was before, except more unpleasant.

José sat in the yard after a hard day's work in the heat of the sun. Louisa, one his sisters, came out. She said, "he wants you. Pulto." She spat out his name. "He wants you now."

"Why me?"

"He didn't say. You'll find him sitting in Papa's chair." She turned and left, flicking her long brown hair behind her.

José got up and went into the farmhouse. He went into the living quarters where the head Dream Fighter sat. Pulto had a scarred and sallow face and a sneer.

"You called me?" José enquired.

"You are going on a road trip," stated Pulto in a deep voice.

"Why? What for?"

Pulto signalled to the other two soldiers. They came forward and put a hessian sack over José's head. He felt like a rabbit in a trap. He exclaimed and complained bitterly.

"Now be silent or we'll have to beat you," explained Pulto, calmly.

The next thing he felt was one of the men grab him round the middle. He was carried into the back of a pickup truck and rolled onto the metal flooring. They left him there for a while.

"You are bad men. I hate you!" shouted José. The sack muffled his cries and if anyone heard him they left him alone.

Later on he felt the truck shake as the engine started. Very soon they were bumping down the long driveway that led out of the farm. The vehicle rounded a turn, rolling his body to the left. José slammed into the side of the open truck and groaned.

Chapter 25

Magda, Paulo Kowalski's mother, liked to make him Pierogi: dumplings with ground meat inside. Today she put them in a soup for him. She sat and watched him proudly as he ate them.

He'd been studying very hard and would one day be a successful English teacher. An inspiration to many. She needed to feed him well. She was so glad he was not a manual labourer, a coal miner like her late husband.

"You are so handsome, Paulo," she said. "Why don't you have a girlfriend?"

"Ma," he complained. "I need to concentrate on my studies. Girls are bad news." He glanced at her from under his thick eyebrows. He had short black hair and podgy cheeks with large pink lips. Sometimes he wore black-rimmed glasses but not today.

A plastic yellow tablecloth covered the kitchen table. Paulo hated it, but his mother insisted on it because it made it easier to clean up. And she was invariably the one who cleaned up.

He picked up his glass which was sitting on a cream-coloured lace doily: one his mother had woven herself. In the middle of the table was a huge arrangement of yellow and white flowers. There was another one on the counter nearby.

Paulo took a sip of iced water and asked his mother to fetch him some pepper for his soup. Happy to oblige, the large matriarch went off to the store cupboard in the adjoining room.

But today there were unexpected guests at the Kowalski house in Katowice, southern Poland. The Dream Fighters kicked down the front door, finding the lock flimsier than expected.

Magda rushed back into the kitchen to see the men drag her boy away. She ran out of the house in pursuit, screaming threats at them. She bounded down the steps of the house to the car but it was too late. The car's taillights flashed as they carried Paulo down the road, into the night.

°°°°°*12345*°°°°°

The visitors had moved on and Ndege returned to his home. It had been the most amazing day of his life. From the house he could still see the angel towering above the crater. Its semi-transparent white robe shimmered from the crater floor up to the clouds. But the angel's face was turned away, looking towards the other side of the crater.

As well as meeting his new friends, and regaining his lost finger, he had also seen a talking lion and danced by the lake to save the world. It was definitely the best day of his life.

His parents came home after dark. They didn't want to hear about his adventures and couldn't see the angel when he pointed it out to them. Instead, they treated him as though he had lost his mind. They didn't even want to hear about his finger.

It was clear they were tired from travelling to Arusha and back. They'd lugged the new furniture into the car and now they had to unload it. Consequently, they had little time to listen to his silly tales. So, he quietly helped them by carrying the drawers and drawer handles. He would try again in the morning, once they had eaten some food and rested.

It was a warm night and Ndege found it hard to sleep. Tossing and turning in his bed, he thought about the amazing angelic being that stood just down the road.

In the middle of the night, his father opened the door to his bedroom, whispering loudly, "There are two men here for you.

192

They say they are your friends. A couple of tough guys by the look of them. I told them to wait outside. It is late to have friends call for you, Andwele."

Ndege quickly became fully awake. He threw off his sheet. "Caleb and Micah!" he said excitedly, running downstairs in his boxer shorts.

But his father had opened the door to the enemy. Instead of Caleb and Micah he saw two men dressed in leather armour. They had brown sashes across their chests. They found it easy to carry him off because he was so small and light. There was nothing his father could do to stop them. They killed him on the doorstep with a dagger.

His father's eyes bulged as he clutched his chest and watched them carry off his child.

°°°°°12345°°°°°

Jia Li had been on her guard ever since she was attacked by the bat. It left her with an incredibly painful wound and a missing thumb. She was also left with terrible nightmares. Sometimes she was chased by wolves across the mountain tops. They would catch her and chew at her flesh. Other times she outran them but still they pursued her.

But she also had good dreams of a warrior king. His name was Rescuer. His face was kind and his eyes blazed like stars. He rode a pale horse and a platinum circle crowned his head. He cared for her and called her into friendship with him.

So when the men in armour appeared at the door of her house, she was ready. And so were her friends: Ri who was fiercely protective of his crew, Cheng the only other man in the house, and her fellow sisters Ancoo and Lin with the flame-red hair.

"Visitors," said Ancoo, running from the kitchen into the main area where they often gathered to read books and chat. She shuffled in her slippers as she moved her slight frame between the rooms. Her hoop earrings swung as she moved.

Ri was ready instantly. He grabbed a long knife and crept stealthily out through the back of the house. Jia Li knew what to do. She went up to her room and closed the door. The other girls did the same. Jia Li glanced out of the window. Her bedroom overlooked the kitchen where the front door was located. She saw two men standing there, stocky warriors dressed in dark leather. They looked around them, waiting. She spotted sword hilts at their sides. Her community knew all the villagers on either side and they knew instinctively that these men had travelled a long distance to get here. They were strangers in these parts and they meant harm, not good.

She watched Ri appear and challenge them. Immediately they drew their swords. Their expressions were fierce, unaccommodating. The two men battled with her friend. The clash of swords rose up to her. It lasted for several minutes. Then one of the warriors ran him through with his sword. Ri screamed and fell to the ground. The armoured man finished him off. Jia Li put her hands to her face. These men were killing machines. She knew deep down it was her they were looking for.

Brave and beautiful, Jia Li stood tall. She took her coat from the rack and went downstairs. No one else needed to die today.

°°°°°12345°°°°°

Samyaza flew on ahead of his army leaving them to ravage Austria and then Germany. He crossed the English Channel with ease, climbing high into the sky like a Messerschmitt preparing to drop its payload onto British soil. It was night-time again and he floated beneath the curve of the moon.

Meanwhile, he communicated with Kumiko.

"I'll be with you soon," he said, projecting himself as her gorgeous surfer boy. She loved it when he popped in on her but tonight she was weary.

"That's what you said last time. And the time before," she moaned.

194

"This time I mean it. Give me an hour. I'll be there at Lytescote."

"Really Sammy? You're really on your way this time? I'll get to meet you in the flesh!"

"You will get to meet me in the flesh, as you say," said Samyaza humorously. He made the surfer wink at Kumiko and she melted.

"I'll wear something nice," she said.

"I'll look forward to it."

An hour later, the fallen angel flew over the shores of southern England. He swooped down on Griffton Cliff, briefly visited the stone head and looked across the city. Snarling, he observed the destruction in the valley below. He could see a few burnt out buildings. It was a start. Lights were on in some of the offices and houses, but the city mostly lay in darkness.

He spread his wings and swooped down over the big house with its angular roof and chimneystacks. Landing near the octagonal gate house, he drew himself up to his full height. His form was tall and bony with black corrugated wings and a face half eaten by fire or maggots. He smelt sickly, rotten.

Taking in the mansion, he smiled then snarled. The front of the house was floodlit and the old bricks and window frames glowed under the glare of the lights. He made a low appreciative noise. It was time to meet Kumiko, his queen. He marched towards the front door and knocked loudly three times with a clawed fist.

A broad Dream Fighter opened the door and fell back in surprise. Samyaza pushed him away and strode in. Kumiko stood waiting in the grand entrance hall. On the wall above her was the oil painting of the Prince Regent.

She wore a black slinky dress, black eyeliner and cherry-red lipstick. Her long black hair was down, flowing over her shoulders. As he entered the building, she recoiled.

"Ah, my Kumiko," growled Samyaza.

"Who are you?" she asked, confused.

"It's me, Sammy. Samyaza, your love. Your king and your companion."

"No!" she exhaled. "It can't be. You look so different. Your face."

"Appearances can be deceptive. Are you ready to take my hand and rule the world by my side?"

She stared at him with her eyes wide and her mouth open. "I can never be with you," she declared.

Samyaza looked at her long and hard. "Have it your way," he rumbled. The demon ruler sprang at her, hoisting her up with his long arm and stretching out his wings. Rising up several feet into the air, he hurled her at the painting with supernatural force. Her body hit the canvas with a hard crack and slid down along the back wall. Kumiko lay, slumped in a heap at the bottom of the wall, staring in horror at Samyaza and groaning.

He closed his wings and walked past her with heavy footsteps, leaving her broken on the floor.

After he left, slowly – agonisingly slowly – Kumiko pulled herself along the wooden floor. She winced as she put one arm in front of the other to drag her painful torso towards the door. As she slithered, she said, "What have I done? Oh, what have I done?"

ooooo*12345*ooooo

Rachel sulked in the semi-darkness. She sat still and hugged her knees, flicking her hair out of her eyes. She was in a metal container: a cube large enough for her to stand up and walk around but that was all. It smelled dank and rusty. The air inside was room temperature: neither hot nor cold.

Dull light filtered through the round holes in the ceiling. Her rucksack and coat were missing. They left her a crust of bread and a flask of water. Earlier, her captors had allowed her to use the toilet blindfolded. But they hurried her along, which she did not appreciate.

Her head hurt from where they had hit her when they snatched her from the mountainside. They only had to do that once. She understood and played dead after that. She allowed them to take her, the pigs. She wondered again how Lake and her father were.

Had they been taken or killed? Her guards wouldn't answer any of the questions she screamed at them.

The container started to vibrate and she heard the hum of an engine. A few minutes later the air pressure in her ears changed and she felt a weight on her body. Flight. She shut her eyes, drained of adrenalin.

Soon, she curled up into a foetal ball, exhausted and small. After that she saw only the black void of sleep.

Chapter 26

Someone was knocking on the door. Lake roused himself from a deep sleep. There it was again. A knocking at the door. Lake groaned. He remembered everything. Eddie was dead. Rachel was taken. He was lying in a remote lodge in the mountains of Bhutan, of all places. He didn't have a car. He didn't have a helicopter. He didn't have anything except a small fire, a bed and some nondescript dry foodstuff.

Then he gasped. Do murderers knock? Or do they just kick the door down and shoot you point blank in the face? Whoever was knocking was very persistent.

The cold air outside his covers was a shock to his system. The room had grown so cold without the heat of the fire. He tried to peep through the window nearest the door but all he could see was white snow, try as he might to crane his neck to get a better look.

Reluctantly, Lake shuffled over and undid the lock. It was a simple affair: a shard of dowel that swivelled down to secure the wooden door.

He took a deep breath and opened up his temporary home to the visitor. Standing before him was a muscular man with long white hair and an open face. His expression was clean and radiated peace. The man was in his early thirties. He smiled at Lake, confidently holding his gaze. On his head was a crown, a simple band of platinum.

"You know who I am, don't you?"

Lake looked away and began to cry.

"Oh, that's okay. A lot of people do that. Would you like me to come in?"

Lake nodded. He turned and went inside, allowing the Rescuer King to follow him and close the door after them.

"I have some food for us to eat. Why don't you wash your face and hands while I set it all up?"

Lake nodded again and plodded over to the sink. The wonderful aroma of hot food filled the air. When he turned around, Lake's eyes became round saucers.

"Is that what I think it is?"

"Hungry?"

"What have you got there? This is amazing. I love burgers. And fries too!" Lake struggled to comprehend the hot burgers, huge bowl of French fries, coleslaw, salads and fizzy drinks laid before him on the table.

"I'm hallucinating, right? You're not really here. Nor is this delicious food." He picked up a chip and nibbled at the end. "This slice of deep-fried potato here. It's not real. None of it is. Lake pulled himself down on a chair and started to eat one of the burgers, realising he was ravenous.

"Are you going to have any?" he asked, and then apologised for speaking with his mouth full.

"I'm very happy to eat with you, Lake." The Rescuer sat down on the other chair and poured Lake a glass of ginger ale. Lake was delighted. It was exactly what he would have chosen.

"This tastes really good. Thank you so much," said Lake, remembering his manners. The Rescuer joined him in eating and they munched in silence for a while.

Eventually, he slowed down. "You're really here," he commented stupidly.

"Yes, Lake, I'm here in the flesh."

"I'm not crazy?"

"That's right."

"Wow." Lake sat back and stared at his visitor. But in an instant, he was suddenly overwhelmed with sadness for Eddie and Rachel and his predicament.

"Eddie's dead," he said quietly.

"Yes."

"Why did you let him get killed?" Lake sniffed. "Why didn't you stop it happening?"

The Rescuer looked at him compassionately for a long time. Then he said, "I love Eddie Race. It is true that in this world, Eddie is no longer with you. But this world is a blink of an eye. It seems long to you, with its troubles and triumphs, its struggles and choices. And its evil. But in the context of eternity, it is the ticking of a second, the flutter of a wing. Eddie has passed out of time but he is alive forever now. He is with me in the heavenly realms."

Lake tried to take in what he was hearing. He nodded once he had computed it all. "Rachel's going to be devastated," he said quietly. "Is she going to be all right?" he added.

"Yes. She will grieve and I will be with her and my Dunamis will comfort her. Rachel is more resilient than you think."

"Who is the Dunamis?"

"He is my spirit. The spirit of truth and the power of the Creator."

"The Creator Rachel talks about?"

"I am one with the Creator, my Father, and also the Dunamis."

Lake opened his mouth to ask another question but the Rescuer said, "In your lifetime, there are some questions to which you will receive an answer and some that you may not. Two hundred and fifty light-years away, in the constellation of Ursa Major, I threw a set of stars into the air. There are five stars – two binary stars and a lone companion and they orbit a single point. The distance between those stars is further than Pluto to the Sun. Do you know the gas content of each of those stars? Are you aware of how many planets spin in that star system?"

Lake shook his head and sat back in his chair.

"Do you know that in this vast and complex universe, I have chosen you, Lake, to eat with? I love you, Lake, and I'm proud of you. I delight in you because of who you are. Nothing you do could make me love you any more or any less. I have counted the hairs on your head and numbered your days."

Lake's eyes were wet with tears. The Rescuer's words filled his head.

"You are so precious to me. There is nothing you have done that can put me off you. I know all of your strengths and your secret desires. Your thoughts, your deeds – good and bad – your regrets and also your potential. And I love you with a fierce and loyal love. My desire is to know you and be known by you. I want to help you to be the best Lake Emerson you can be, day by day. I want to walk with you and converse with you. I want to help you to love people and carry hope in your heart. Are you ready to follow me?"

Lake nodded, looking down. He felt the strong presence of the King. The being before him was so pure and powerful, full of goodness and love. He felt like a spotlight was shining on his heart, revealing all of the dark spots.

"I've done so much I am ashamed of," Lake declared. "So many bad things I've thought. I hurt people in school. Bullied them. I never really loved anyone. Just myself. There were times when I didn't stick up for people. Just walked on by."

As Lake spoke, other dark memories came to mind. His secret vices and the things that haunted him in the night. He felt ashamed. Repulsed by himself and his past. In the presence of the King, he felt like his life was a pile of filthy rags.

"It's all right, Lake," said the Rescuer, putting his hand on Lake's arm. The King's face was burning brightly like a halogen lamp. His head and hair were white like wool, as white as snow, and his eyes were like blazing fire. It was difficult to make out his features. "Give it all to me. Let me take it all and burn it up. And in its place, I will give you my purity. New clothes. Freedom. Forgiveness. Peace. New life."

Lake closed his eyes and the fire of the Dunamis fell on him, flooding his veins. The Rescuer continued to breathe words of restoration over him. He could no longer hear them but they went deep into his heart.

°°°°°12345°°°°°

Lake awoke from a long sleep. It was still daytime. He lay on the bed in the wooden house in the mountains. He felt different: rejuvenated. His sense of desperation had gone, though he knew that Eddie's body still lay outside in the snow.

"Come outside. It's time," said the Dunamis.

"I can hear you!" Lake exclaimed. He scrambled over to the sink to wash his face. Looking up at the mirror, he saw that his hair was white like Rachel and Eddie's. Like Caleb Noble's. He laughed spontaneously. He tousled it with his fingers.

"Yeah, this is good," he said out loud. He put on his coat and snatched up his pack. He looked around his temporary abode for the final time. He wanted to remember the place where he had encountered the Rescuer. Then, filled with peace and purpose, he went outside.

A very light snow was falling. The flakes were almost imperceptible.

"Where do I go, Dunamis?" He still felt the aftermath of his transformation: the change that brought him into a close relationship with the Rescuer and his Dunamis. His body buzzed with electricity and his senses were heightened.

"Up. This way."

Lake climbed up the mountain path. The air was crisp and cold. His strength had returned to his legs and his feet were firm on the steep slope. He paused to enjoy the vista that opened up around him: rollercoaster peaks and troughs; dazzling inclines and astounding drops.

The Dunamis took him a different way from before, although the path began in the same place. This time, he wove around a thin track that rose sharply. It required him to scramble upwards using his hands and staying close to the ground. He climbed and climbed, breathing in the thin air. The steep ascent put him on a plateau high above the lodge. There was far more ice up here and a view of the top of the nearby mountains. Their white curves and angular facets cut into the light blue sky. Black and grey stripes and patches covered the lower parts of the mountains.

"Woah," Lake commented. He stood with his hands on his hips, watching his breath create foggy white clouds in the air.

"It's time to activate the Protector of the Air," said the Dunamis.

"What, now? What do I do?" asked Lake, slightly alarmed.

"The least of the least will dance before the King in the air, pure and free."

"That's me isn't it?" laughed Lake. "You're talking about me, aren't you? I am the least of the least. The least likely to follow the Rescuer. The least of the least because the universe is so big and I'm a tiny ant on this massive mountain: I get it! And he's made me pure and free. I can feel it."

Lake started to jig with joy. "Thank you. I am so grateful. Rescuer King. It's my pleasure to dance before you because of what you've done for me. I don't know how this is all going to work out but I trust you, like Eddie said. To know you is to trust you. And I do."

Lake danced on the mountainside, slipping and sliding, feeling crazy but dancing with all his might. The ground beneath his feet began to shake. Lake stopped and stared.

From the depths of the valley basin below he watched a gigantic white figure grow up from the ground. Stretching towards the sky like a tree, the shimmering angel grew in height and bulk. As it rose to reach the limit of its towering height, it lifted up two great white wings. Lightning flashed through them. The being wore clothing made of filmy light. It turned its face and countenance away from the mountain and stood to attention. Lake's mind reeled.

The Air Protector had joined the battle for the human race.

Something had changed in the mezzanine. The angels knew it. The demons knew it. Something momentous had happened and the rules had changed. The stone heads no longer worked. The heads had come from the Initiation; from the mountains. Used by the enemy to travel and transport their prisoners, and harnessed by the army of light to accomplish their purposes, the stone heads were now dead.

Mattatron discovered the change first. One minute, the powerful angel of light was standing with his comrades in the mezzanine. The next minute his location shifted and he stood in the middle of a yellow desert. Green cacti and bushes poked out of the ground and the sky was blue, not purple. A small white crescent hung in the pale blue sky.

A group of Angel Hunters were the second to find out. They were just about to pounce on an unsuspecting angel in the mezzanine scrubland. As they jumped down from the high rocks, they suddenly found themselves in a building full of people and shelves stacked with food. Their victim disappeared, leaving them in this alien place. Confused, the creatures roared at the top of their lungs, angry at the enemy's trickery.

The war had entered a new phase.

°°°°°*5fingers*°°°°°

OUT IN 2016

The final instalment in the 5fingers series

Follow Joshua Raven's blog at www.joshuaraven.com
Twitter: @RavenWrites
Facebook: Joshua Raven Author
Pinterest: Joshua Raven 5fingers

ABOUT THE AUTHOR

Joshua Raven lives in the South of England with his wife and three children. He loves to travel and write about places he's seen and places in his head. He's been to some of the locations in the 5fingers books: including Tanzania, Bali, New York, Katowice and Chengdu – but not Griffton, Bolivia, Jura or Sand Island – not yet anyway! Joshua has enjoyed over twenty years as an international journalist and editor, interviewing leading figures in business and technology, and writing for publications and businesses across the globe. 5fingers: rescue is his fourth commercial novel and his tenth major work of fiction. He blogs at www.joshuaraven.com and Tweets at @RavenWrites